# Barred

Aella C Grey

# The Book:

"Knowing right from wrong, or good from bad is easy, Ms. Leclair. Standing up for what is right, and good, no matter the cost? That's the hard part."

Azura Leclair thought escaping her abusive father meant a fresh start for her family. Now, as she juggles working as a receptionist at Blackwell Law Firm and keeping her brother Cole out of trouble, she stumbles upon a disturbing truth—the school is violating students' constitutional rights.

Desperate for help in a race against time, she turns to Vassago, a powerful attorney from Gloam Legal and her boss's biggest rival.

Threats close in, and as danger lurks at every turn, Azura is forced to question everything and everyone around her. In a world where morality is as elusive as a shadow on the wall, she must decide if standing up for what's right is worth losing everything she holds dear.

Will Azura save her brother and his future? Find out in Barred, a paranormal romance, and book two of the Prince of Hell series.

# The Author:

Aella C Grey is an author hailing from Winnipeg, MB, Canada, currently residing in the sunny state of Florida. When she's not immersed in the world of writing, Aella indulges in her other passions, such as playing video games, diving into captivating books, and cherishing quality time with her beloved dog and supportive husband.

With a vivid imagination and a deep appreciation for storytelling, Aella brings her unique perspective to the realm of fiction. Her love for literature and interactive entertainment has fueled her creative endeavors, inspiring her to craft compelling narratives that transport readers to captivating worlds.

Aella's writing draws readers in with dynamic characters, intriguing plots, and a touch of magic. Whether she's exploring mystical realms or delving into the complexities of the human experience, her stories are infused with emotion, suspense, and a dash of the unexpected.

Stay connected with Aella C. Grey through her website to discover more about her upcoming works, behind-the-scenes insights, and to join her on thrilling literary adventures.

# Barred

by

Aella C Grey

Aella C Grey

1. Edition, 2025



Aella C Grey

# Table of Contents

# Important

Much like the Unbroken, the Prince of Hell series has ties to real world problems, which some readers may find uncomfortable. As with all fictional books, the relationships are special in their own way, with characters that have their own personalities and flaws. None of my writing is meant to diminish the seriousness of what individuals have gone through in their lives, nor is my writing meant to demean religion in any way, shape or form.

# Trigger warnings:

Anxiety, Attempted Murder, Blood, Child Abuse, Cults, Character Death, Demons, Gore, Grieving, Hospitalization, Kidnapping, Murder, Profanity, Religion, Religious Trauma, Touch Aversion, Secret Society, Sexually Explicit Scenes, Violence

# Glossary

There are multiple pronunciations for these words, especially given different dialects, so please see the phonetic pronunciation below as intended for this series.

Azura (Ah-zu-rah)
Leclair (Leh-cl-air)
Vassago (Vah-sah-go)
Gloam (Gl-oh-m)
Raphael (Rah-fai-el)
Seir (See-er)
Oriana (Oh-ree-ah-nuh)
Arrenault (Arr-eh-n-alt)
Merrick (Meh-rr-ick)
Theodric (Thee-aw-d-rick)
Stolas (Sto-l-ahs)
Orobas (Oh-roh-bas)

# Chapter 1

*Not to be dramatic, but God, I **hate** hospitals.*

The fluorescent lights reflect off the polished linoleum floor as distant beeps sound out beyond the double set doors where they wheeled mom through hours ago.

Even without the stress or anxiety of worrying about her, there's something exhausting about endlessly sitting in a waiting room that makes me want to curl up in one of these chairs and sleep like Cole is.

I glance to where he lies on the medium-sized bench. His overgrown brown hair is a mess, with his head awkwardly resting on his forearm at an angle. Drool has pooled under where his mouth hangs open, and even from here I can hear his soft snore fill the air.

*Teenagers can sleep anywhere, I guess.*

*Probably best for him to rest while he can.*

My eyes slide shut as I lean my head back against the wall, hearing another door open and footsteps echo into the eerily quiet waiting room.

"Azura Leclair?"

I jolt upright, my gaze landing on a doctor holding a clipboard against his chest. With no one else but us in the waiting room, his eyes are glued to me with an uncertainty in his expression that makes my gut twist.

*Shit. This can't be good news.*

***Please** be good news.*

My legs tremble as I push off the chair. The fake leather sticks to the bare skin at the back of my thighs and my heart feels as if it could beat out of my throat with each cautious step closer to the doctor.

"My name is Dr. Harper, a surgical oncologist with Providence Medical Institute." His eyes flick to where Cole still snores behind me and my palms sweat. "I wanted to let you know that your mother's surgery went as well as it could. She's in critical condition because of the amount of transfusions she needed, and we had to put her on a ventilator. She's in intensive care for now until we can stabilize her."

Critical condition. A ventilator. Intensive care. *I guess it could be worse. She could be dead.*

My mind goes blank, and I nod as he continues. "We removed most of the mass, but there was extensive damage to her internal organs. We removed a large portion of her large intestine because of how far the cancer had spread from her liver."

*Cancer.*

*Metastasized.*

I filter through all her symptoms and behaviors over the past few months with a bitter note of regret.

Every wince when she moved, how tender she said her back was, and how she always rubbed the area near her ribs. How much weight she'd lost and the nausea she'd had. So many nights I'd wake up to the sound of her retching down the hall.

The number of times I just thought she'd caught a bug from Cole at school, or had gotten a bad flu.

Dr. Harper searches my face for a moment, and I just nod for him to continue as my body goes numb. "We'll keep her under our care for the next few days to give her fluids and medications to keep her comfortable as she recovers. I—" He pauses, and my heart drops into my stomach as I brace for the inevitable. "I don't want to put this kind of worry onto your shoulders, but this cancer is aggressive.

With your mom's current state, it could be weeks or months at this point with treatment."

The tears that had formed in my eyes fall loose down my cheeks, and I nod, feeling my bangs shift against my cheeks with the movement.

*I knew something was wrong, but for it to be cancer? Aggressive cancer that's metastasized?*

*All our lives, mom never showed weakness, but to have this thing slowly killing her this whole time?*

*How did I not see it?*

*Why didn't she go get it checked out sooner?*

Dr. Harper's hand moves to my shoulder, and it takes everything in me to not react. I want to crawl out of my own skin, to scream for him to let go, and I can hardly pay attention to the pained expression he wears as he looks at Cole again. "I'd suggest for you and your little brother to go home and get some sleep for now. We will call you to come back if her condition worsens."

The lump in my throat grows, and my voice is hardly more than a whisper as his attention turns to me once more.

"Thank you, Dr. Harper."

He gestures to the woman just down the hall, sitting behind a desk as she types information into the computer. "Lucille will call you at the number on file if anything happens."

I nod again, feeling more numb as the doctor gives my shoulder a firm squeeze that makes me want to rage before he heads toward Lucille. Glancing over at Cole, he looks so peaceful that I decide against waking him up yet. He doesn't deserve to have his world flipped upside down yet.

My mind is a mess of thoughts as Dr. Harper murmurs something to Lucille, and I make my way over as she turns to me with a warm smile.

"Ms. Leclair." She tilts her head slightly, and her red curls dance against her collarbone. "Can you look at this paper and just let me know if all the details are correct?"

I glance at Cole, still fast asleep on the couch before scanning over the page.

*Dartmouth street. Home number. Cell.*

Blowing out a breath, I nod. "It's all good."

Lucille smiles warmly again. "Great. We'll call your cell first if we have any updates on your mom's condition or need authorization for treatment. Visiting hours for the ICU are between noon and four PM for twenty minutes, with one visitor maximum. Check in at the front desk when you come back, and they'll make sure you're all taken care of."

She slides a paper over that has the same visiting hours noted down, and I couldn't be more thankful for it as I struggle to remember a fraction of what she said.

"Thanks." I murmur before walking over to Cole as if my body is on autopilot, and I sober at the thought of going home soon. Leaning over, I give his shoulder a gentle shake, and he jolts up. "Cole, let's go home."

Even in his half asleep state, he frowns and rubs his eyes. "What about mom?"

There's a lump in my throat, and I swallow hard against it as I hold myself together by a thread. "She's in recovery, and we need to rest. We'll be back to visit tomorrow or something."

My gut twists. I know it's a lie.

Cole has his first day of high school in the morning, and I need to work. There's not a chance in hell we can make it after no sleep.

"We can't see her now?"

The desperation in his voice makes my chest tight as I shake my head. "Visitation hours aren't until tomorrow afternoon, and it's midnight."

He rubs his eyes and pushes to his feet unsteadily, somehow still an inch taller than me at fourteen when he stands up straight

"Come on." I whisper, hooking my arm into his and leading him down the hallway. "We'll be back before we know it."

# Chapter 2

"You can let my three o'clock in, Azura."

Theodric's voice comes through the speaker of the phone, and even though he can't see me, I nod absently as the call disconnects. I've hardly pushed to my feet when I hear his muffled but irritated voice through the wall, and I step out from behind my desk.

"Mrs. Merrick?" The older bleach-blonde haired woman with a pencil skirt and a fancy blouse stands up, clutching a stack of papers to her chest. "Mr. Blackwell will see you now."

She looks warm to the untrained eye, but there's a coldness to her that even her smile can't reach as I guide her to Theodric's office. I don't know much about Blackwell's clients, and the one thing I do know about her is that she came into a lot of money when her husband died.

A cursory glance at her file once told me she owns a bunch of property in the state, which she regularly sees Blackwell to discuss as she looks to increase her wealth. Our heels click repetitively against the wood floor, breaking the stillness in the air as I pull the door open and gesture for her to go inside.

Theodric Blackwell, the owner of Blackwell Law, and the best attorney in town, stands as she walks toward him, and he shakes her hand.

Before he can angrily tell me to leave like he usually does, I close the door, hearing his muffled voice echo through the wall as I return to the front desk once more.

I've been working in this quiet law firm since I turned eighteen, going on four years now, and for the last two, Blackwell's attitude has progressively gotten worse. For a while, I thought it was because of the separation between him and his wife. But when Gloria said they parted on good terms, that theory went out the window.

The other possibility is that the only competition to Blackwell has effectively snagged most of our new cases from us as of recent. They're not even located in Rennensberg. I don't know much about the person who owns the practice, but that's the other plausible reason for his poor attitude.

Sitting down once more, I pull my phone from my purse only to see missed texts from Cole. My heart falls into my stomach.

Dropping him off for his first day of high school was hard enough without mom being there. I don't need to open them to know he's struggling after visiting mom alone today because I wasn't able to leave work long enough.

Guilt hangs heavily over me like a dark rain cloud as I scroll through his messages.

**Cole:** Just got to the hospital. The nurse is walking me over to the ICU now. Visitation is only 10 minutes today. So bullshit.

**Cole:** She's not even awake. She looks so fucking weak and small, Az. They had all these cords attached to her.

**Cole:** I wish you could've come w me. I'm at class now.

**Cole:** When r u coming home?

My chest tightens, and my fingers fly over the screen as I cautiously listen for any movement from Blackwell's office.

**Azura:** I'll be home in an hour and a half. Blackwell's been in a mood. See you soon.

My mind wanders to what it must have been like for him to cab by himself during his lunch break, and another fresh wave of guilt sags my shoulders.

Even at fourteen, Cole's been through more than any kid ever should have been.

I was eight by the time Cole was born, and already in a dark place. Our deadbeat dad, Jeffrey Leclair, was a raging alcoholic who didn't even try to work through his vices.

By the age of six, I lost my innocence to that piece of shit, and it didn't stop until I reached the ripe old age of fourteen. Clearly, that was too old for him. When Cole was about to turn seven, the man who was supposed to protect us shifted his attention off me, and onto my baby brother.

I had just turned thirteen when I ran at him with a kitchen knife after finding him with Cole.

That was the first time he had hospitalized me, but it wasn't the last. I ended up in the ER a handful more times with broken bones because I fought that asshole with everything I had.

During the first hospitalization, mom finally realized the man she thought she could trust had done unspeakable things while she was working two jobs to make ends meet.

That didn't stop Jeffrey, though.

No, that bastard just continued his abuse whenever she was away.

But I'll never forget the night we finally left. It rained the entire day, as if the heavens themselves wept for us. Mom had been hiding important things in secret places for months in preparation, and we just waited for the opportunity.

Cole was ten when Jeffrey molested him for the last time, and I had spent the night nursing both of our wounds. He'd drank himself into a stupor, and mom had come home two hours early only to find us huddled in a closet after crying ourselves to sleep.

We didn't learn until later that she had crushed up a sleeping pill and put it into his–*nearly empty*–whiskey bottle as he slept. When I told her that could have killed him, she just shrugged and said that she hoped it did.

The night we escaped, we snuck out with only what we could carry, and walked down the street to an awaiting cab.

That's how we moved here to Rennensberg. The drive felt like an eternity, but soon enough, we found ourselves sitting in a motel, nervously looking at the door every five minutes.

After a week, I worried that he'd find us, no matter how many times mom had reassured me she'd covered her tracks well.

After two months of sending out resumes and applying for jobs, mom spoke with the dean at our local church, and he'd contacted a few colleagues before I'd finally landed a handful of interviews.

I was about to accept a job bagging groceries at a nearby store when Gloria, the receptionist from Blackwell's office called me.

So, for four years we've been here, building new lives while doing our best to heal.

If anything, the time spent in Rennensberg has only brought us closer even though I'm out of school and mom's still working to pay the bills.

I hear the chairs in Blackwell's office shift slightly and glance at the clock.

*Still half an hour left before his meeting ends.*

My mind wanders back to Cole as I absently sort through some files. Over the past four years, the frequency of his nightmares have lessened, and he finally decided it was time to sleep in his own room a little over a year ago.

He started to work out in the school gym after class throughout middle years, even though they'd called a few times to make sure he was allowed. It seemed to be a good outlet for him.

Lately, he's even been talking about joining the school football team, and I can't help but feel proud at how much he's grown.

Cole might just be my little brother, but for so long we were each other's rock, and safe place.

*Although, he's not so little anymore.*

My phone vibrates as I glance down at it, and a quiet murmur sounds out from Blackwell's office.

**Cole:** Drive safe Az. I'll be home late.

Footsteps fill the air, and I slide my phone away seconds before the door opens, and Mrs. Merrick walks out, smoothing her skirt as she does.

I'm watching her disappear into the parking lot when Blackwell's voice fills the air. "I'll close up tonight, Azura."

Nearly jumping out of my skin, I nod. "Sure. Thank you, Mr. Blackwell." I file away the paperwork I was sorting, gather my things and hurry out the door.

In the past four years I've worked for Blackwell, there hasn't been a single day when he's let me off early. With my mom's condition and having no meetings for the rest of the afternoon, I have to imagine he's doing this to be nice.

*Maybe he's not as moody as I thought.*

# Chapter 3

By the time I get home with groceries in hand, the house is still dark.

An uncomfortable quiet fills the space as I methodically put the groceries away, and my mind wanders to mom.

Earlier this morning, the hospital had called to tell me she was still in ICU, but her vitals were showing improvement. The nurse still seemed optimistic and said she may regain consciousness any day.

It seemed far-fetched for her to recover that fast after such an intensive surgery. But hey, who am I to argue when it comes to healthcare?

I absently shut the fridge door and turn, nearly jumping out of my skin when Cole stands a foot away from me. "Oh, Jesus."

He scoffs. "I hate when you do that."

My eyes widen in disbelief. "Me? You're the one sneaking up on people!"

He just shrugs, stepping closer to pull me into a tight hug. "Sneaking and saying Jesus' name like that is **not** the same thing."

I suppress an eye roll and return his embrace, still reeling from the jump scare. It takes a moment, but I finally relax as he ruffles my hair, like **I'm** the teenager between us.

With him already inches taller than me, at a glance, it might seem like it.

For my entire life, Cole and mom have been the only people I've been able to get remotely close to without getting angry or anxious. There was once a girl I was acquaintances with in high school who hugged me from behind, and I landed myself in the principal's office after having a meltdown.

I can't blame her, not entirely.

It's not like she had any idea that it would trigger me. We'd never talked about it.

The school reiterated that she needs consent before making such advances in the future, and I got off free with a warning and a handful of counseling appointments.

Pulling away, I glance at the clock with a frown. "Why were you so late coming home?"

He just shrugs again, opening the fridge and grabbing a bottle of water. "Stayed late to talk to someone. Are you going to see mom tomorrow?"

I nod. "Yeah, Blackwell has no meeting around lunchtime, so I'll go then."

Cole grabs a takeout container from the fridge and starts piling food onto a plate. "Did the hospital call you?"

My palms grow slick as I grab a bottle of water from the fridge too and crack it open. "Yeah. They said her bloodwork has improved. She might wake up any day."

He puts the plate into the microwave and presses a button before a constant hum fills the air. "Do they know what it is or why she had to have surgery?"

My heart drops into my stomach, feeling as if it's weighed down by two tonnes of lead, and when his brown eyes meet mine, I know I can't keep it from him.

*He deserves to know the truth.*

"It's cancer, Cole." My voice is only a whisper as he blinks at me.

"That can't be—"

"I know. I thought the same at first, but the signs were there. We just didn't see them." *I just didn't see them.*

His throat bobs, and the microwave beeps once, twice, three times.

I know he's going to blame himself. Hell, I've been doing the same, but there's no way we could have known. She needed to see a doctor much sooner and there's nothing that will change that fact.

"Eat your food, Cole. We'll see her tomorrow."

He seems to snap out of whatever daze he was in as he nods, snagging his food from the microwave before making his way down the hall.

*Tomorrow will be a better day.*

*It has to be.*

After putting the rest of the groceries away and grabbing a handful of baby carrots from the fridge, I quietly make my way down the hall to the front room, pausing when I get to Cole's doorway.

It's half ajar, and I can barely see him kneeling at the edge of his bed, elbows nestled into the covers, with his hands clasped in front of his face.

From here, I can see his brows knitted together, and I don't miss the streaks pouring from his closed eyes as he whispers. It's almost loud enough for me to hear, so I take a cautious step to the doorway and lean in.

"... Archangel Raphael, I beg thee, please help my mother. Lord, I pray you can protect her and heal her, heavenly Father, giver of life and health..."

I lean back to give him privacy, feeling a twist in my stomach as I walk silently to the front room. It's not out of the ordinary for him to pray, but the desperation in his hushed voice is what's tightening my chest the most.

When dad started to abuse us, we turned fully to our faith to get through it with each other. In that closet, when we would cry ourselves to sleep, it was after we'd spent hours chanting prayers over and over and over. We'd sneak into each other's rooms every night, using a knock only the other would recognize before praying next to the bed. By the time we ran away, there was never a time we were without a bible.

That also made the transition to Rennensberg easier, because the town is filled with people of faith. The schools allow time for prayer, and the businesses donate to our local church, Rennensberg Covenant–formerly known as Holy Alliance. The changeover happened just before we moved here, when a neighboring town's mega church, Divine Covenant, had bought out ours. When we moved, all the signs were still being switched over.

The change was the talk of the town, and most people sang praises of how much good Divine Covenant had done for our neighboring town Gracefield. With most places being closed on Sundays, and everything else taken into consideration, it's not out of line to say that most people in our town are God-fearing, bible toting folk.

Admittedly, my faith waned over the years, and although I would judge no one for the God they pray to, or if they pray at all, I silently observe it all with a note of cynicism.

*Because where was God in all of this?*

*Where was He when I lost my innocence for the first time?*

*Where was He when my baby brother lost his?*

*Where was He the second, third, or twentieth time we were both defiled?*

I sigh deeply, throwing myself onto the couch with a huff.

*No.*

*If there was a God, He's just as fucked up as we are for knowing all the evil in this world, for having the power to help, and yet choosing not to.*

# Chapter 4

*A few days later*

This has arguably been the longest week of my life.

Putting a stack of files into the cabinet, it's safe to say that Blackwell has been a menace every day, even calling during the single, ten-minute weekday visit with mom. She's still unconscious, but her blood work has been improving gradually, so the doctors are still hopeful.

Rolling my chair back to the desk, my mind replays each night when I'd walk down the hall to go to sleep, hearing Cole pray in his room. Listening to his soft sobs fill the air has been maddening. Each time made it harder and harder to not be angry that his pleas go unanswered.

On Saturday, we finally managed to visit mom for a full twenty minutes, but during that time, Cole held mom's limp hand at the side of her bed, talking to her while I held his other hand in mine.

He told her about school, the bullies he'd seen, the people he'd met, and his new friends.

All things he'd normally never say out loud, but among the beeps of the hospital room and his desperation for her to wake up, I think it's all he felt like he could control.

After spending Sunday curled up together on the couch with snacks, I'd offered to watch one of our classics, but the sadness on his face when he agreed made me realize it would only remind him of mom.

So we spent the rest of the night watching some random movies he picked that I hardly paid any attention to because my mind kept wandering back to work and all the things I needed to do today.

And now that they're all done, as I stare at the time on my phone, four-thirty has never looked better.

I had originally taken this job because it paid well for not needing any prior experience, and I figured a law firm was a good place to gain some.

*Little did I realize this job would suck the very soul out of me.*

Sure, Blackwell is a lawyer and a viciously good one at that, but the man squeezes every penny out of his clients. He seems more inclined to help those more well-off than others. He only takes cases he knows he can win, and his overall attitude has made him a terror to work for in the past couple of years.

The clock ticks by another minute, and I gather my things to go home.

If nothing else, this job has helped me save a small nest egg of cash for a rainy day, and that alone makes me grateful.

The clock changes again, and I grab my purse, pausing when my phone vibrates loudly against the desk.

An unknown number displays on the screen, and I frown, picking the phone up to put it against my ear.

"Hello?"

Static sounds out before a female voice comes through. "Hello, is this Ms. Leclair?"

My heart drops. Could this be the hospital?

"This is."

"Hi, Ms. Leclair. I'm Mrs. Jorsen from Rennensberg High school. We've been trying to get ahold of Mrs. Leclair, but it seems like she's unavailable. I'm calling to see if you can come get Cole from the school since you're the next emergency contact listed."

Dread washes over me like a wave of ice. "Is he okay? What happened?"

There's a long moment of silence on the line, and with every passing second, I feel like I'm going to go insane if she doesn't say something.

"He's just fine. He got detention today and is required to remain here two hours after class."

My jaw drops. "For what?" My voice comes out shrill, and I clear my throat.

Mrs. Jorsen, however, keeps her voice steady as she responds. "During prayer this morning, Cole declined from participating, but it is mandatory for everyone to take part." I frown, and my mouth drops open, but she continues. "What time will you be here?" Her tone is impatient, and I can't help but wonder if it's because of the content of the call or because she's supposed to be off work.

"I'll be there in thirty minutes."

It only takes me twenty-five minutes to get to Rennensberg High School, and I navigate to the principal's office. The winding corridors throw me back to my time in the education system, and it's a bittersweet memory.

*School was an escape, but it never lasted long enough.*

Turning the last corner, I step into a main office where a woman sits behind the desk, typing at her computer. Assuming she's Mrs. Jorsen, I approach the desk, and she smiles warmly.

"Hi, how can I help you?"

Returning her smile, I force it maybe a little too much. "I'm here to speak with someone about Cole Leclair? I'm his older sister, Azura."

"Ah, yes. Right this way."

She rolls her chair back and pushes to her feet before walking around the front of the desk. "Cole is in the other room with his counterpart. They're nearly done with their detention."

I frown as she crosses her arms and stares at the closed door a few feet away. "I'm confused. He got detention why, again?"

My gaze flicks between her and the door as she purses her lips. "Prayer is the holiest of time. That being disrupted is absolutely unacceptable."

Unacceptable? Mandatory prayer? What kind of school **is** this?

My mouth drops open to respond just as the door opens, and Cole's silhouette fills the entryway. His head lifts and his eyes lock with mine as guilt flashes across his face.

Another student walks out behind him, looking even more dejected as she passes by us in a hurry.

Mrs. Jorsen watches the girl with a frown before gesturing to the exit. "I look forward to not seeing you in this office again, Mr. Leclair. Now, if you'll excuse me, I must speak with Mr. Humphrey."

Her heels click as she paces into the next room, and I glance at Cole, who just shakes his head.

"Alright, kiddo. Let's go home."

We're finally in the car, and I put it into drive, glancing every few seconds at Cole. His face is solemn as he stares out the window, and my gut twists.

"Do you want to talk about it?" I ask, feeling the tension in the car grow with each passing second.

His silence isn't reassuring at all, and I spare another glance before turning my eyes back to the road ahead. From what I can see, he's deep in thought, but Cole's always been one to pull back into himself rather than talk about his issues.

"You can tell—"

"She isn't religious."

My mouth snaps shut, and I frown. "Who?" The moment the word leaves my lips, I remember the young girl hurrying past us from the office.

He shifts next to me, rubbing his palms together in his lap. "Her name is Anna. She just transferred in from out of town, and she doesn't know anything. They made her pray, and she didn't know what to say, so she stayed quiet. They gave her warnings, and she just started crying."

Something tells me I know how this is going to play out already, but I ask anyway. "So, what happened?"

Cole's hand flexes and tightens on his thigh. "They were about to suspend her when I stood up and said I don't know any of the prayers, either. That's when they gave us detention after school."

I nod, picturing it in my head as I turn the last corner to the house. "I'm proud of you for standing up for her."

In my peripherals, he just shrugs. "It was the right thing to do."

"So, what is she going to do for future classes?"

I hear him sigh. "I'm going to teach it to her so she can say it quietly and they can leave her alone."

The grin that creeps across my face is genuine, and I bark a laugh. "Look at you, sneaky as can be. She's a lucky girl." When he rolls his eyes, I just laugh harder. "I'm serious. She's found a good friend. Not everyone would do that."

We pull up to the house, and he's out the door in an instant, pacing the steps and pulling out his key as I follow him inside.

"Someone has to do it. This is the only place I've had to do mandatory prayer before. It sucks."

I frown. "Wait, so you mean to tell me that everyone in the class **has** to participate?"

Cole nods, and his throat bobs as he swallows. "Yeah. Each day, every student has to do prayer for the first thirty minutes of class and the first thirty when we're back from lunch. If we don't, they can expel us."

*That can't be right. It's not legal to force mandatory prayer.*

Oblivious to my confusion, Cole continues on. "They give us three passes during the year, and each time we don't join in prayer, they give detention. Once you've used all three passes, on the fourth, you're expelled permanently."

"That has to be a mistake. It's a public school—"

Cole groans, leaning forward to rub his face with his palms. "I don't know, Az. They made us sign some waiver on our first day."

My face pales, and I turn to him with a shrill voice. "You signed something without telling me?"

He shrugs, and it takes all my restraint not to get more upset. "I didn't think it was that important."

This means he already has one mark against his record, and he has two more before he's expelled.

A plethora of what-if's run through my mind and anxiety builds in my chest. "Okay, okay. Alright. I'll talk to the school tomorrow and see what we can do about it. Just... don't get into any more trouble, okay?"

Cole flashes a toothy grin. "I can't make any promises, Az. You know that."

*He's going to be the death of me someday.*

I roll my eyes and pace further down the hallway to the kitchen to start dinner. "Behave or else." My warning is half-heartedly a joke, but deep down inside, there's a part of me begging him to be careful.

His footsteps pause by the doorway to his bedroom. "Oh, hey, Az?" I halt my movements to glance at him, seeing apprehension clear on his face. "Mrs. Boray gave me a permission slip for you to sign for a week-long field trip to Father Arrenault's campground. Can I go?"

My chest tightens at the thought of being away from him for so long, but I nod. "Yeah, that's fine. Just put it on the counter before you go to bed, and I'll sign it."

He grins and disappears from sight, but all I can think of is how I'm going to clear his name.

*This has to have been some kind of mistake.*

*Surely. Right?*

# Chapter 5

"Ms. Leclair. How can I help you today?"

Rennensberg High School principal Mr. Humphrey, a short and stout man surrounded by a chaotic mess of papers, sits behind his oversized solid oak desk. His beady brown eyes are so dark they might as well be black, and he clasps his hands in front of his face, leveling me with a deadpan stare.

Painfully aware that I'm basically a child in his eyes, I emulate my best impression of Blackwell that I can muster. Straightening my back and pulling my shoulders down, my hands clasp in front of me, and I take a centering breath.

"Mr. Humphrey, thank you for agreeing to meet with me on such short notice. I'd like to discuss a recent incident that occurred with my younger brother, Cole Leclair."

Humphrey says nothing, but gestures for me to go on, and I feel my palms grow clammy.

"It is my understanding that he abstained from participating in prayer to—"

Humphrey shakes his head and cuts me off mid-sentence. "Quite frankly, Ms. Leclair, it doesn't matter why he abstained." He chews the last word out as if it tastes bitter, with his lips curled in disgust. "He signed an oath, and he's expected to keep up his end of it. We do not allow rule breakers in our school, Ms. Leclair. Surely, you can understand that, yes?"

My jaw clenches as my teeth grind together. "Right, but his punishment seems a little drastic considering what he did to earn it."

I watch the principal stand to his full height, still hardly more than an inch taller than me as his face turns a bright shade of red, and he leans his palms onto the desk.

The action sends a rush of adrenaline through me, and I struggle to ignore it. To stay focused.

"To be quite honest, Ms. Leclair, I don't care why he abstained or whether it deserved the level of punishment he received. He broke the rules and that cannot simply be ignored. If we make an exception for one, we must make an exception for all."

Frustration coats my veins, and I cross my arms over my chest. "So you're telling me that there's no way to rectify this?"

My eyes are wide, and my brows pull together tight as he shakes his head. *Does this guy have no empathy? No compassion?*

"I'm afraid not, Ms. Leclair. Cole will just have to be diligent to not incur any additional detentions. Has he not learned from his mistakes?"

Adrenaline pumps through my body, and my voice gets louder as I speak. "How in the world can you be forcing students to conform to religion? What if they don't believe in your God? What then?"

The reddish tinge to his skin turns a more vibrant hue of crimson as he grips the desk, and his knuckles go pale as I wonder how fast I'd need to sprint to the door if he tries anything.

"How dare you insinuate He is simply 'something' to be believed in." Humphrey pushes off the desk and stalks closer. "You should really be more careful about how you address these sensitive topics, Ms. Leclair. It would be a shame for anyone to assume the wrong things about your statements in the eyes of the Lord."

My eyes narrow on him, and instead of making him clarify his thinly veiled threat, I swallow down my pride.

"I'll take that into consideration. Have the day you deserve, Mr. Humphrey." I whirl around, keeping my strides confident as I leave the office and make directly for my car. I hardly make it to the hall-way as my arms tremble.

*I fucking hate confrontation.*

Years of abuse from Jeffrey made me more inclined to flight rather than fight unless Cole is involved, and I exhale a ragged breath when I get to the entrance of the school.

*There has to be some way to clear his name. It's insane that he even had to do detention in the first place. This has to break some sort of law...*

That's when it hits me. *This breaches the first amendment.*

My lips curl into a smile as I cross the parking lot, and I formulate a plan as I head back to work.


By the time I've made it to Blackwell's office, I'm deep in thought about what my next steps need to be.

Clearly, I need to find a lawyer, preferably one that I know or has taken an interest in the case.

*Maybe also one who doesn't cost an arm and a leg.*

The issue is that Blackwell Law is the only law firm in town, and he's so unpredictable, not to mention expensive.

I'm in a daze, going through the motions as I settle into my desk and begin pulling the first few files out for appointments. I barely spend five minutes prepping when I realize I've zoned out and disor-ganized the files by appointment time, then I sigh deeply.

"Did you not sleep well, Ms. Leclair, or are you sighing loud enough to wake the dead for a reason?" Blackwell's voice jolts me from my daze, and the file I had in my grip falls to the floor.

"I—shit," I scramble to the floor to gather the papers, and trepida-tion builds in my veins.

*If anyone knows what to do, it would be Blackwell.*

Swallowing against the lump in my throat, I grasp the papers and push to my feet, my gaze sliding to Blackwell's beady eyes.

"If there was an organization suspected to be breaching one of the amendments... would you ever take that case?"

He frowns, and the crease in his forehead turns into a thick line. "Speak your mind, Leclair. I don't have time for hypothetical or vague scenarios." The edge to his voice only serves to send adrenaline pumping through my veins.

"I recently discovered that a government funded organization is breaching the first amendment."

Blackwell's eyebrow quirks up as if he suddenly becomes interested. "What organization is this?"

My heart thunders as I find my voice, which only comes out as little more than a whisper. "Rennensberg High School."

His face suddenly falls flat, turning serious before fading into something reminiscent of a scowl. "You don't know what you're talking about. How the hell do you think they're breaching an amendment?"

A wave of embarrassment washes over me, and my eyes widen. "I'm certain they are—"

"Drop it, Leclair!" Blackwell suddenly barks, and I flinch as his face turns a light shade of pink. "Rennensberg High School has always been known as a stand-up institution, and has a track record of being thorough." He levels me with a deadpan stare that makes my pulse rage in my ears. "Make accusations at your own risk, but do not dare do such a thing with the name of my firm attached to it."

My heart drops. "You don't even want to hear—"

He waves dismissively and disappears into his office. "There's no case there, Azura. Leave it alone. I'll expect your resignation on my desk the day you bring a case against them for something so ridiculous."

I hear the front door swing open as the first appointment of the morning arrives, and I slide back into my chair. My fingers tremble as I thumb through the files, half in a daze.

*There's no way this is it. Cole is just screwed, then? Blackwell is the only firm in town, so if he won't represent us, what's to say anyone else will?*

*There has to be some way.*

The lump in my throat grows, and I pull the file for the first appointment to the front.

*This is going to be a long day.*

# Chapter 6

My feet stomp angrily against the linoleum as the reflection of the fluorescent lights reflects off the surface, and I breeze past the receptionist's desk.

"Ms. Leclair—"

"Where is he?" I look at the empty chairs lining the walls, and my blood pressure rises when Cole isn't there.

*Fight response activated.*

"He is still in detention, and will be for another twenty minutes, Ms. Leclair."

I glare daggers at Mrs. Jorsen, feeling a heightened sense of panic that he now has two out of three detentions.

"There has to be some mistake, Mrs. Jorsen."

Her lip curls, and I glance at the door, seeing Cole on the other side in the center of the room, writing something into a notepad.

"There is no mistake. Mr. Leclair needs to learn to respect the rules."

My arms fold across my chest, and I tilt my head to look at her. "What did he do?"

She just sighs. "It's once again what he didn't do. It seems your brother has taken to a rather rebellious young lady, and when she doesn't partake in our mandatory prayer, he does not either."

My jaw clenches, and a hard boulder of resignation settles in my stomach.

*I need to hold the school accountable, and I need to do it soon.*

*All of this will be for nothing if he gets expelled from the only highschool in town before I can take them to court.*

"Okay." I say, taking a seat on one of the waiting room chairs as her eyes widen. "This won't happen again."

*It **can't** happen again.*


It feels like an eternity has passed by the time Anna and Cole step out of the room with their heads hanging dejectedly.

They jolt when my voice cuts through the air with more authority than intended. "You two, outside. Now."

I wordlessly lead the way to the parking lot, pausing by the car and glancing around before turning myself loose.

"What the hell do you two think you're doing?"

Cole's eyes widen as he glances between us nervously. "What—"

My palms jut out between us to halt his words. "I already know your explanation from the first time you both got detention. What was the reason this time? Are you not practicing?"

Cole glances at Anna, and she fiddles her thumbs together, with her long hair falling forward as she looks at her feet.

I sigh. "Listen, I don't care that you're not taking part, but you're both going to be expelled within a month at this rate. I'm going to find someone to help us, but I can't do that if you're both expelled before I can hold the school accountable."

Anna blinks at me. "How are you going to do that?"

My shit-eating grin holds more confidence than I feel as I hold the car door open for Cole. "I'm going to find a lawyer and we're going to take them to court."

*I just need to find a lawyer that's willing to represent me, and not charge me an arm and a leg.*

*Something tells me that's easier said than done.*

~

My fingers rhythmically drum the table as I wait for the search results to load. The first five attorneys are all sponsored ads from Blackwell Law, and I scroll down to see a handful of suggestions showing near me which have long since closed down.

Supposedly over the last twenty-five years, Blackwell has beaten out all competition except one. Given his prevalence, it's not surprising that his ads take over half of a page of search results, but as I scroll, my heart sinks when there's only three other options, all of which are in neighboring rural towns like ours, in the middle of nowhere.

The air conditioning clicks on, and I jot down all three numbers before inhaling deeply to calm my nerves.

*Norem Legal, a one hour and fifty-minute drive.*

*Tomias Law Firm, two hours and twenty minutes away.*

*And Gloam Legal, Blackwell's biggest competitor, a whopping three and a half hours from here.*

I sigh deeply, dialing out the first number, and it rings twice before a woman's nasally voice fills the air from the speaker.

"Norem Legal services, can you hold please?"

I nod, even though she can't see me. "Sure."

After a few long minutes, the hold music cuts out. "Thank you for holding. How can I help you today?"

Subconsciously, I lean forward in my chair and fiddle with my pen. "Hi. I'm Azura Leclair, and I'm hoping to make an appointment with someone about an organization breaching the first amendment."

There's a long pause of silence on the line. "One moment."

Hold music plays for another few minutes before the woman comes back on the line. "Sorry hun, we don't have the capacity to take on that kind of case right now. Please feel free to reach out to another firm, though."

The edge in her tone has me frowning as she disconnects, not even waiting for my response. A small part of me can't help but wonder if she disapproves of the case.

*Or maybe I'm just imagining things.*

I dial the next number, and it beeps before an automated message sounds out. "The number you have dialed is not in service..."

A feeling somewhere between resignation and hopelessness settles into my bones. My hands tremble as I dial the last number, and it rings once, twice, three times.

*I don't want to beg Blackwell to help me with this, but what else am I supposed to do?*

The phone continues to ring, and I'm about to hang up in frustration when the deep tenor of a man's voice fills the air.

"You've reached Gloam Legal. Who am I speaking with?"

The tremor in my voice makes me cringe as I give my name, and the chill from the air conditioning sends a shiver down my spine.

"How can I help you, Azura Leclair?"

My chest tightens as I breathe out my response, feeling as if my last chance to help Cole is currently circling the drain. "I currently live in Rennensberg, and I'm hoping to meet with someone about an organization in town that is breaching the first amendment."

There's a long pause, and I'm already bracing for an outright denial as the male voice on the other line comes through once more. "How exactly is this organization breaching the first amendment?"

*Okay, don't freak out. Blackwell asked the same thing.*

My heart thunders, and adrenaline pumps through my veins. "Uh, well, it's a public school, and they're forcing students to take part in mandatory prayer, while punishing and even expelling students who do not participate."

The man on the other line huffs a surprised laugh. "Rennensberg? Well, I'm damned."

I frown, hearing honking in the background before a car door opens and closes.

"Well, what?"

The man's background goes silent until I hear the rumble of an engine from his end of the line.

*Is this guy a receptionist playing hooky? What the hell is going on?*

The man's voice fills the air once more, and it sounds like I'm connected to a Bluetooth device with how the audio has changed. "You said Rennensberg, correct?"

I nod, resting my head in my hands as I brace for the denial. "Yes, that's correct. Is that a problem?" *God, I hope not.*

He huffs a laugh. "Not at all. That's just somewhat far. I mean the drive to get here would be—"

"Three hours and thirty minutes."

The line is silent again after my interruption, and I worry that I've offended him as I blurt out. "I don't mind–" My heart pounds, but I can't lose this one chance I have. Not now. "I'll drive there and back, I just need help. Please..."

Another one, two, and three long seconds passes, and I feel like I can't breathe as I wait.

"I have an opening tomorrow at three-thirty, which, I understand if it's short notice for you, but otherwise I'm booked out for weeks."

I blink. "You're the attorney!?" There's a pause after my sudden outburst before his genuine, rich laughter rings out, and my eyes widen.

*If this guy is the attorney, I'm so fucked.*

*He doesn't have someone to take his calls like Blackwell, and his unprofessionalism in comparison screams that he's going to get chewed up and spit out if he takes this case against Rennensberg High School.*

*But I don't really have a choice. Beggars can't be choosers.*

The man collects himself and sighs as if that was the funniest thing he's heard all day. "Should I pencil you in for tomorrow, Azura Leclair?"

Rubbing my palms against my eyes, I nod even though he can't see me. "Please. I'll be there tomorrow at three-thirty."

The rhythmic ticking of a turn signal sounds out from the speaker. "Wonderful. Bring everything you can for evidence, and names of those involved. I look forward to meeting you Ms. Leclair."

I blow out a breath, already wondering how the hell I'm going to manage to leave work early with the mood Blackwell has been in.

"I look forward to meeting you as well... What was your name? Is it... Mr. Gloam?"

The man's hearty laughter rings out again, and my cheeks burn.

*I assumed his company name was his.*

*Isn't that what most lawyers and firms do? Market their names?*

The man clears his throat after his laughter calms, but I can still hear the smile on his face, as if he's still silently laughing.

"My name is Vassago, Ms. Leclair."

I frown. "Well, it'll be nice to meet you Mr.–ah, Vassago. See you tomorrow."

The line disconnects, and I stare at the piece of paper covered in scribbled numbers and notes before glancing at the exhausted list of legal firms on the screen.

*God, I hope this works.*

# Chapter 7

The incessant beeping of medical equipment from the surrounding rooms feels like it's drilling holes in my brain as we sit next to mom's bed.

With a tear running down his face, Cole leans in, holding her hand, whispering hushed words of encouragement and pleading for her to wake up.

My throat constricts, and I drag my gaze from him to keep myself composed.

Calling in sick to work had been the right thing to do this morning, since only an hour later the nurse had called, asking us to come see mom and speak with the doctor at eleven thirty.

So after driving Cole to school with the promise of not getting detention, it wasn't long after that I was picking him up to go to the hospital to see mom.

A soft knock on the door echoes into the room before Dr. Harper, and who I'm assuming is one of three doctors on shift steps inside.

"Ms. Leclair?"

I push to my feet and head toward the doorway. My heart gallops in my chest a mile per minute as my nerves fray with each step toward them.

The doctor glances at Cole before his eyes land on me once more. "An SDU is going to bring your mom to a general medical-surgical ward on the east wing of the hospital today. She's stable, and no longer exhibiting signs of immediate concern, so we're hoping her condition will continue to get better." My heart soars, but I feel the same elation fall when his expression remains solemn. "Even though we are hopeful, I still need to make sure you understand she could take a turn for the worst. Just know we're prepared if it comes to that."

I swallow hard, giving him a nod.

Dr. Harper offers a clipboard and pen between us with a forced smile. "If you can, please sign here to give your approval for the transition unit to move her."

My trembling hand moves to take the pen, and I scribble an illegible signature before he tucks the clipboard under his arm.

"Once she's in the general medical ward, visiting hours are from ten AM to four PM." He glances between the three of us, and his foot moves backward as he goes to leave. "I won't take up any more of your time."

He slips out the door with the shift doctor in tow, and I make my way back to Cole in a daze. Seeing mom's pale and weak figure slumped on the bed beside him, her oily hair clinging to her forehead with sunken eyes.

*She's the strongest woman I've ever met, and to think that cancer will claim her in the end.*

*I suppose it's always **something** that takes us.*

Refusing to hold on to those dark thoughts, I shove them away into the recesses of my mind.

"What did the doctor say?"

My gaze flicks at Cole's red-brimmed eyes, and I choke down any sadness or negativity, if only for his sake.

"He said she's doing well, and they're going to move her to the general medical ward since she no longer needs intensive care." Cole's worry is palpable as he nods, and I wrap an arm around his shoulder. "That's a good thing, kiddo. Next step is for her to wake up and start demanding to work again."

He laughs under his breath before his chest rumbles even louder, and soon, I grin with him.

Another soft knock sounds out at the door, and a nurse peeks her head in. "Sorry guys, visiting time is up."

Cole leans over to press a kiss to mom's temple, and I do the same before following him to the door with a heavy heart.

"You said you have an appointment today?"

I nod, navigating us through the winding hallways to the parking lot. "Yeah, after I drop you off, I'm heading to an appointment out of town. I don't know what time I'll be back though, so Elena next door is going to pick you up from school and hang out at the house with you for a few hours."

Cole groans, tilting his head back in disapproval. "I know she's mom's friend, but she's so annoying."

I bite back a smile as I shrug. "Tough times, kid."

Three hours of this drive have dragged on like days, and my finger-tips thrum the wheel in time to the song playing from my phone's playlist.

That's the one good thing about long car rides. Music always makes it better.

By the time I get to the rural town of Gracefield, my heart is a war drum as it ricochets against my chest, and every now and again it feels like it could crawl from my throat.

I don't know if it's meeting this attorney or going against Blackwell that has me so nervous, but I'm beyond ready to get this over with.

Seeing my final turn up ahead on the map to Gloam Legal, I finally pass a building with tall trees lined up in front before I see the turn for the parking lot.

I take the corner, and my eyes widen.

The building is large, dark-grey, and mostly made of windows. Spanning two stories high, it's much wider than Blackwell's office, which, in comparison, is more like a rented office space in a larger strip mall.

*Could this guy really be legit? Maybe he just shares this space with other attorneys or companies.*

I hadn't seen any attorney names on the search results, so it's hard to say for sure.

There's only a handful of cars in the parking lot, and my eyes narrow on the expensive looking grey Mustang parked on the side of the building.

I blow out a breath, gathering my miniscule file of notes, a handwritten testimony from Cole, and a recount of both occurrences.

My attention flicks to the door as a woman in a pencil skirt and blouse steps out, navigating on the uneven parking lot surface with ease on her slender, four-inch heels.

I glance down at my leggings and sweatshirt, feeling out of place in comparison, but I shove that thought away.

*Nope. There's nothing better than authenticity, and that's what Vassago is getting.*

Swallowing my nerves, I clutch my things to my chest and head inside.

If I thought the outside was all windows, the inside is entirely made of glass. Most of the panes separating the rooms are frosted, with designs etched into the surface and art that covers most of it. Birds, butterflies, and various other animals, mountains, lakes, forests.

By the time I make it to the front desk, I'm still taking in the awe of everything around me when the receptionist tilts her head and smiles warmly.

"Hello! Welcome to Gloam Legal. What can we do for you today?"

Blinking at her, I manage a tight smile even through my frayed nerves. "I'm here to see Vassago at three-thirty."

*So he has a receptionist, but he answers his calls?*

Something about this entire thing puts me slightly on edge, but I don't know if I'm just imagining it because I'm already hanging on a thread with the entire reason I'm here.

The receptionist types something into her computer before glancing up at me with a warm smile. "Right this way, Ms. Leclair."

She pushes to her feet and walks around the desk to lead me down a long hallway. We cut right once, then twice, before taking the elevator to the next floor in silence.

The elevator pings, and the doors open wide as she leads me to the windows at the end of the hall. The moment she turns to the right, she gestures to a room. "Here you are, Ms. Leclair."

Murmuring a quiet thank you, she leaves me in the doorway and I step inside, feeling my pulse rage in my ears.

The butterflies in my stomach feel more like a hoard of cats trying to claw their way out of my body. Goosebumps break out over my skin, my limbs tingle as my palms grow more clammy, and I don't know what has me suddenly so nervous.

"Ah, Ms. Leclair." My gaze tracks the sound of the deep voice to the tall, dirty-blonde haired man with a neatly styled high taper fade seated behind the desk as he pushes to his feet. His dark grey, well-tailored suit is form fitting, and I feel my pulse hike as he makes his way over. "It's a pleasure to meet you."

He offers his hand between us, and I automatically slide my palm into his as he gives it a gentle squeeze. I'm uncertain if it's my anxiety at the contact or his overwhelming presence, but the air gets caught in my lungs as he unintentionally towers over me. The moment lasts mere seconds but feels like an eternity, and he releases my hand, gesturing to the chair facing his desk.

My eyes gravitate to his hand, and I spot the tattoos peering out from the cuff of his sleeve that stretch to his fingers.

Blackwell would have scoffed at them, calling him unprofessional, but it's all I can do to ignore the way my stomach tumbles as I follow his gesture.

"Please, make yourself comfortable."

"Ah, thank you." I murmur, feeling breathless as I slide into the seat. He moves to sit across from me, and the air of authority around him threatens to suffocate everything in existence as he leans back, clasping his tattooed, ring covered hands over his torso.

*Is this really the same person I spoke with on the phone?*

"So, tell me about this school."

*Never mind.*

I blow out a breath, feeling the weight of this entire ordeal settling heavily on my shoulders.

"My little brother got detention a little under a week ago. He and the school both stated it was because he didn't recite prayers with the rest of the class. According to him, he was doing so because his classmate isn't religious and doesn't know any of the group prayers."

Swallowing hard, Vassago's bright grey eyes look almost near-white as they drop to my throat before returning to meet mine once more.

I rub my palms together nervously as a fresh wave of goosebumps break out over my body. "When my little brother abstained from participating, he and his classmate were both given detention. I later found out that the school had my brother sign a waiver to agree to a set of terms that if he gets detention three times, upon the fourth time, he will be expelled from Rennensberg High School entirely."

By the time I'm done, my voice is hardly a whisper, and my chest squeezes when Vassago looks at me with a level of understanding in his expression that takes me by surprise.

His lips part, and my gaze drops to his mouth. "How many times has he received detention?"

My stomach churns uncomfortably at the thought. "Twice."

Vassago leans forward, placing his elbows on the desk as his hands clasps in front of his face thoughtfully. "Well, as of this very moment, this definitely appears to fit a breach of the first amendment. As I'm sure you know public schools are state funded, and so forcing students to conform to any religion in order to attend is strictly prohibited. At least, for now, anyway."

"For now?"

His eyes remain trained on me, and I feel as though I'm extremely out of my element.

"There's a case currently with the supreme court that's not much different than your situation. That case's outcome could determine how the court handles yours."

I nod, handing over the file of evidence and supporting documents as he looks them over. He's quiet as he scans through it all, seeming to stare at one page for a moment with a distant look. When he seems to focus on the page once more, his brows pinch together for a breath of a moment.

Finally, he places the paperwork down before tilting his head toward me with a smile. "Right, well... I'd be happy to represent you in this case, Ms. Leclair."

Emotion clogs my throat, because we haven't even gotten to the hard part. My voice is hardly audible as my gaze drops to the floor.

*God, I hate dealing with money.*

"How much is this going to cost?" When he doesn't immediately answer, I ramble on as if I need to explain myself further. "My mother is in the hospital and I don't know if she'll make it, so it's just me and my brother... and my salary alone hardly covers our living costs..."

He leans back once more, looking at me pensively. "I do not do pro bono work, Ms. Leclair."

I nod, feeling tears brim my eyes even though I knew this was going to happen. This would be a long and difficult case where he'd have to be thorough. *That takes time, and time is money.*

"But, in this case, I think I can make an exception."

I freeze. My jaw goes slack, and I blink at him as he grins, flashing his pristine white teeth as I contemplate pinching myself.

"Why—?" I cringe at my accusatory tone, but he just pushes to his feet, walking around the desk to lean back against it.

If he seemed tall before, he's infinitely taller now with the way he dominates the space over where I sit, and I have to tilt my head up just to look at him. His bright grey eyes peer down at me from beneath dark lashes as nervous butterflies soar through my body.

The way he studies me makes me want to squirm. "As the best legal representative in this state, the easy and selfish thing for me to do would be to give you a price you cannot afford and force you to submit to the whims of evangelical zealots. I'd expect most firms would opt to take that route."

He thumbs the ring on his index finger in circles as he continues. "However, I believe in doing the right thing. And sometimes doing the right thing means it's the difficult, cost ineffective and outlandish path filled with fraught and challenges. Knowing right from wrong, or good from bad, is easy, Ms. Leclair. Standing up for what is right, and good, no matter the cost? That's the hard part."

I hold his gaze, which seems strangely bright as he searches my face, and my voice is hardly above a whisper as I look at the man who may just become my saviour after all.

"So, what do we do next?" I ask, leaning back in my chair and the tension finally starts to leave my shoulders.

"Well, we have a strong case considering everything you've told me. Seeing as we're in the initial phase right now, I'll need to meet with a handful of individuals from the school, as well as your little brother, to question them about recent events. Once I've met with everyone involved and submitted a Notice to Produce to the school, we should be good to file and ready ourselves for a lengthy trial."

My chest swells with what I can only describe as hope, and I bite down on the inside of my cheek to keep my eyes from welling up. "Thank you."

His expression is soft as a slight smile graces his features. "You've got nothing to thank me for yet, Ms. Leclair."

My cheeks burn. "What else do you need from me, then? Anything?" I'm overly aware that my emphasis on the last word comes out breathy, and I just tell myself it's because he's being so generous.

*It has nothing to do with the air of authority that surrounds him.*
*Clearly.*

He looks over his shoulder thoughtfully at the papers strewn across his desk before moving to his seat and lifting a couple. The way he moves seems cautious yet deliberate, and I find myself distracted as he sets them down once more.

"You said your brother got detention already?"

I nod. "Twice."

His brow twitches upward ever so slightly, but he continues to scan over the papers. "Did you speak with the school?"

My hands tighten in my lap and I squeeze them together soothingly. "I did."

His eyes flick up to me and narrow. "And?"

I don't know if it's just my perception, but the air feels thick, like there's an overarching tension that could snap at any second as he watches me expectantly.

"I was told that it would be a shame for anyone to find out about my statements about the Lord and assume the wrong thing about who I am."

There's a stillness in Vassago as he takes in my statement with the tensing of his jaw the only sign of malcontent. "So he threatened you."

The way he says it sends an icy shiver down my spine, but I can't deny it because that's exactly what it was.

I nod. "Indirectly."

Vassago leans back in his chair, using his thumb to rub the stubble along his jawline. "What do you do for work, Ms. Leclair?"

I wince at the constant formality. "Call me Azura please, or just Az. Ms. Leclair feels too... adulty..."

Vassago chuckles under his breath, and my cheeks burn. "What do you do for work, Azura?"

Hearing my first name said in person is like velvet to my ears, and I realize it was a mistake.

I never want to hear my name said any other way, now.

"I'm a receptionist for Blackwell Law Firm."

His eyes widen, and I brace myself for the question. "I'm assuming you already tried to inquire with the legal representatives who work there?"

I nod slightly. "Yes."

"And?"

My head shakes from side to side. "Blackwell told me to drop it. He said that Rennensberg High School is thorough and there's no case there."

Vassago's jaw ticks again. "I see. So your brother has two strikes against him out of three, someone threatened you, and your employer is involved."

My eyes widen. "I never said Blackwell was—"

He waves his hand dismissively. "He's either complacent or involved. Either way, his inaction speaks louder than any admission he may make."

I watch with rapt attention as he notes something down on a piece of paper and slides it toward me. "Here's my personal cell number. The number you originally dialed only routes to me if my receptionist is busy. I want you to save this in case anything comes up."

I nod, pulling out my phone and plugging in his information into my contacts.

"When you say in case anything comes up, you mean—"

"If **anything** comes up." The seriousness in his voice, and the way it drops lower makes my stomach tumble, and I nod.

"Great. Should I book another time with your receptionist downstairs?"

He shakes his head. "No need. I can pencil you in now." He shuffles his papers to the side and flips open his laptop before typing what could only be a mile per minute.

"How does three weeks sound?"

I nod. "That sounds fine." *Guess I'll be sick twice this month. Sorry, Blackwell.*

Vassago snags a small card from the table, noting a date and time on it before sliding it over the desk to me. He pushes to his feet as I place the card in my purse, and I take that as my queue that we're done.

"Well, Azura. It was a pleasure to meet you, and I look forward to working together."

I follow him to the door, feeling ten times lighter as he pulls the door open, offering his hand toward me. I'm bracing for the negative reaction as my palm slides into his. Nothing happens outside of the butterflies dancing through my core, and he gives it a gentle squeeze as surprise rifles through me.

My entire body warms. "Likewise, Vassago. Thank you for your time today."

By the time I'm following the hallway to the elevators, my mind is half in a daze as I press the button, and I watch the LED by the ceiling go from the first floor to the second.

Now all we can do is wait.

Wait and maybe pray.

# Chapter 8

*One week later...*

Cole's footsteps disappear down the hallway as my cell rings, and I hoist the groceries onto the stove with a grunt, reaching in my pocket as I fumble for it.

In the week since my appointment with Vassago, we've gotten into some semblance of a routine in the days that followed.

Every day I drive Cole to school, every other day he visits mom during lunch, and I pick him up after I'm done with work, or Elena does when she's not working. Truth be told, outside of being worried about mom, it's felt like the universe was finally giving us some reprieve from the chaos it had thrown our way.

I glance down, seeing Providence Medical Center on the screen, and my heart drops as I quickly slide my finger across to answer.

"Hello?"

Static from the speaker rings out before a woman's voice fills the air. "Hello, is this Azura Leclair?"

My pulse is raging in my ears as I nod absently. "Yes, this is."

"My name is Mrs. Brunsword, and I'm a nurse with Providence Medical. I'm calling to let you know that your mother is awake now. She is still being treated in the general medical center, but we wanted to let you know if you wanted to visit, there's a good chance she'll be awake."

I nearly drop my phone as my heart leaps into my throat. "Okay, great. Thank you for telling me. We'll stop by during visiting hours tomorrow."

"Great, we'll see you then. Thank you."

The line disconnects, and I stand there, still half in shock.

*Awake. She's actually awake.*

Blinking furiously at the tears welling in my eyes, I place my phone on the counter with an ache in my chest.

*I need to tell Cole.*


Rhythmic beeping sounds out in time with mom's pulse as we sit next to her bed.

I hardly slept all night knowing we were going to get to see her today, and my mind feels foggy as I watch her eyes flutter shut before straining to open once more.

Whatever drugs they've been giving her to reduce her pain have kept her in and out of consciousness, and judging from the way Cole's face fell, he had different expectations for how today was going to go.

What made it worse was when we first arrived, he talked to her, and she only mumbled gibberish in response before her eyes rolled back in her head.

The gut-wrenching sadness in his expression nearly broke my heart.

After a few minutes he'd stopped trying to hold a conversation and reverted to the usual–talking at her and murmuring what his days have been like, what she would have wanted to see and everything in between.

I honestly don't know how he comes up with so much to say, but somehow he manages.

Before I realize it, our visiting time is up and the nurse ushers us out the door to administer mom's medications. The walk down the hall is quiet, and I feel Cole slide his hand into mine.

It's a subtle gesture, but it's one that speaks a thousand words to me. Whenever Cole felt like his world was shattering, or it was simply becoming too much, he'd always reach out, quite literally.

He'd never ask for anything, never explain what was going on in his mind, but I knew.

My hand squeezes his, and I lead us both to the parking lot without saying another word.

Not because I have nothing to say, but, because there are no words that will make mom healthy again. There's nothing anyone could say that will ease the reality that's crashing down onto both of us.

And that reality is that mom will never be healthy again.

That reality is that the two of us on our own is the new normal.

I know it's not the truth that he wants, but it's the truth, and we're just going to have to figure it out together.

The rest of the drive is quiet, with just the engine rumbling breaking the silence until we pull up to Rennensberg High School.

"See you after class." His voice sounds so small that it makes my throat constrict painfully.

"See you then, kiddo."

I pull away from the school at a snail's pace, my mind wandering to Vassago as I drive back to work.

*Could he still be investigating? I wonder how many people he's spoken to, or what he's uncovered so far.*

A wave of unease flips my stomach, and I chew the inside of my lip.

I know I'm playing with fire by filing a case against them, but this is Cole's future they're toying with.

*Nobody fucks with my little brother and gets away with it.*

By the time I'm at Blackwell's office, a wave of determination has settled deep into my bones, and I know I'm going to have to go through hell to keep their claws out of him.

# Chapter 9

Two appointments have come and gone, and Blackwell's door is closed when my phone vibrates in my purse.

I go to put a file away when it vibrates again and again.

And again.

Frowning, I pull my phone out and unlock the screen, only to see a handful of frantic texts.

**Cole:** Please don't hate me.

**Cole:** I really messed up.

My pulse spikes, and I scroll down to see the first message.

**Cole:** I got detention again.

My eyes stare at his message with dread, mentally recounting all three occurrences like I'm magically going to come up with a different number.

**Azura:** How?

**Cole:** How do you think?

Frustration wells up within me, and my fingers fly over the screen.

**Azura:** We've been over this a million times. How did you get detention still?

**Cole:** Mr. Green changed the mandatory prayer last second, and it was a surprise. I didn't mean to today.

I sigh loudly, leaning my forehead into my palms as tears well in my eyes.

This can't be right. For him to get this many so fast... Something has to be up.

The next one means he's expelled completely.

I blow out a shaky breath, and my hands return to my phone.

**Azura:** Okay. We'll figure this out together. Just... be careful.

Nausea churns my stomach as I find Vassago's phone number in my phone. My thumb hovers over the call button, and I hesitate.

*What can he even do to help?*

*All we can do is file our case and pray it helps.*

*It's not like he can fix this.*

My eyes slide shut, and the tears gathering in my eyes fall to the desk, and I put my head into my palms. A shudder runs through me and my breath hitches as I desperately try to stay quiet as the tears continue to pour down my cheeks.

Desperately trying to cling to something positive, my mind claws for something, anything, but comes up empty, and another shudder wracks through me as a quiet sob crawls out my throat.

"Azura?"

I freeze as Vassago's voice reaches my ears, somehow sounding far away as my gaze drops to my phone.

My tears coat the bottom half off my phone, and I notice the thirty-second timer continuing to count as I sniffle, wiping the tears quickly before picking up my phone.

Not wanting Blackwell to hear my conversation, I hurry outside, placing the wet screen to my ear.

"Hi, Vassago. Um, sorry about that..." Clearing my throat, my voice wavers, and there's a pause on the other end of the line as I try to keep my voice steady. "You asked me to let you know if anything else happens, right?"

"I did—Are you crying?" His tone sounds bothered, and I clear my throat again awkwardly.

"I'm fine. I just wanted to let you know my brother got another detention."

Vassago mutters a curse under his breath. "What happened?"

"I don't have all the details yet, but he texted me to say that his teacher, Mr. Green, changed the mandatory prayer last second, and so he wasn't prepared."

There's a long moment of silence from the other end of the phone, and I'm hardly holding it together.

"What else happened?"

I hesitate, swallowing against the ball of emotions clogging my throat. "That's it, that's all I know."

"I'm not talking about the detention, Azura."

My head shakes from side to side, even though he can't see me. "Nothing. It's fine—"

I'm interrupted by the office door opening and Blackwell peering outside.

"Azura, am I paying you to take personal phone calls?" The red hue of Blackwell's face sends a nervous shiver down my spine.

"I need to go." I whisper hurriedly, and click the end call button before shoving my phone in my pocket.

The moment I get to my desk, Blackwell's glaring at me with a note of suspicion.

"What's gotten into you, Azura?"

I shake my head. "Nothing."

That doesn't convince him though, and he continues on. "You used to be detail oriented, eager, thorough. Now you're calling in sick, using your phone all the time and forgetting things."

The sigh that escapes me comes out more frustrated than intended, forcing me to explain if only to take his attention off of it.

"My mom is dying, my brother is facing detention and possible expulsion, and I'm the sole provider for our household while also trying to support him emotionally. I'm sorry I've inconvenienced you."

Blackwell scoffs. "Inconvenienced me? The only person you're inconveniencing is yourself. Take the afternoon off. When you return, either dedicate yourself to your duties or submit your resignation to me."

Tears blur my vision as I nod, grabbing my purse and hurrying to my car.

*This is all Rennensberg High School's fault.*

*If they didn't have these stupid rules, this stupid oath, and these stupid mandatory prayer sessions, this wouldn't be happening.*

*My baby brother wouldn't be risking his future for nothing.*

I pause at an intersection, torn between turning right to go home, or turning left to go to the school to see Cole.

My pulse picks up, and I yank the wheel to the left, slamming on the accelerator.

*No.*

*This is my baby brother they're fucking with.*

# Chapter 10

It's mere minutes before I pull into the school parking lot, and I've yet to flesh out a single well-thought-out plan.

No, for the entire drive all I thought about was what I want to say to Mr. Humphrey. What I dream of saying to Mr. Green. And lastly, what I desperately want to scream at Mrs. Jorsen.

Putting the car into park, I release a ragged breath before hauling myself inside.

The oppressive fluorescent lights remind me of the hospital, and a wave of sadness washes over me as I'm reminded of how long mom might have left in this world.

My mind is a mess of jumbled thoughts as I storm into the office, passing by Mrs. Jorsen as she surges to her feet, calling after me as I remain singularly focused.

I throw the office door open and take three angry steps inside. "We need to talk, Humphrey."

Humphrey murmurs into his phone before placing it on the receiver, and my chest heaves as adrenaline pumps into my veins.

"What can I do for you, Ms. Leclair?"

My mouth drops open to speak as a familiar voice sounds out right behind me.

"You can begin by explaining why Cole Leclair was given detention." I freeze in place, feeling a hand on the small of my back as Vassago moves to stand slightly in front of me.

Humphrey scoffs, his cheeks turning a light hue of pink. "And who are you?"

Vassago's steps are confident as he approaches the desk, offering his hand between them. "My name is Vassago. I'm the attorney representing the Leclairs."

The way he says it sounds like a threat, and Humphrey must realize this as he suddenly pales, glancing between us with a wild look like he's been trapped.

Vassago flashes a grin and retracts his still empty hand before wiping the cuff of his sleeve absently.

"And what exactly are you representing the Leclairs for?" Humphrey grinds out. The malice in his gaze sends a shiver down my spine as his eyes linger on me.

Almost as if he can sense my discomfort, Vassago steps forward ever so slightly, completely obscuring me from Humphrey's line of sight as he lets out a dark chuckle.

"Well, we can start with clearing up this little miscommunication. It is my understanding that a teacher of yours is responsible for mandatory prayer sessions. Is that correct?"

There's a moment of silence, and I fight the urge to look around Vassago to see Humphrey's reaction.

"That is correct." His response is clipped, pointed and resigned as if he knows he's in a lose-lose situation.

That's when I recognize the trap Vassago has laid for Humphrey is not one that he can just dismiss or avoid so easily.

Vassago shifts in place, crossing his arms over his chest. "What are the expectations for said teachers when it comes to communicating these changes to the students and how long are they given to adapt to the new prayer?"

Even from here, Humphrey's breathing picks up, and I chew the inside of my lip nervously.

"The changes are communicated by email and text at least twenty-four hours ahead of time."

The back of Vassago's head shifts in a nod. "Great. Then you should have no problem showing me the communication that was sent to the students."

My eyebrows shoot up and my heart thumps hard against my chest.

Could it be something so simple?

"You'd have to see Mr. Green for that. I don't keep those records."

There's a long moment of silence, and I see Vassago's head tilt. "And should we find that Mr. Leclair was left off the distribution list?"

Humphrey scoffs. "You won't. That's impossible. Those distributions are pre-set to currently enrolled students."

My heart thunders as Vassago turns, and the first thing I see is how bright red Humphrey's face is.

"Let's go see Mr. Green then."

I turn and head toward the door, feeling the feather-light touch of Vassago's hand at the small of my back, guiding me forward. "I would recommend that you join us, Mr. Humphrey."

The authority in his voice sends a thrill down my spine, but I nearly laugh when footsteps follow us out the door. It only takes a minute to get to Mr. Green's class, and I pause, raising my hand to knock on the door when Vassago reaches past me to twist the knob before pushing it open.

The class is thankfully empty, minus the older man sitting behind a desk near the front of the class. His thick-rimmed glasses sit low on his nose as he reads the paper in front of him, with the bald patch at the crown of his head reflecting the fluorescent lights above.

He raises his head, but before he can say anything, Vassago's deep voice fills the air, and he breezes past me as he makes his way to the desk.

"Ah, Mr. Green. My name is Vassago, and I'm here regarding an incident that occurred today with one of your pupils. I'd like for you to please show me the distribution list for both the email and text blasts which went to the students for today's mandatory prayer."

The way he chews out the last two words makes his disdain for it clear, but he just smiles at the old man as he steps up alongside the desk with Humphrey in tow.

"Marcus, what is the meaning of this?" Green scowls at the three of us before moving to close his laptop.

"Ah—" Vassago grins like a madman, his finger hooked over the top of the laptop as he tuts. "You'll want to comply with this request, I'm afraid."

"Who do you think you are?" Humphrey seethes. "You can't just come in here making demands."

"I'm afraid I can," Vassago sighs wistfully. "You see, it's either that you show me the distribution lists, and they validate that Mr. Leclair was simply lazy or not paying attention, or–and this is an important one, so you'd do well to listen–or, you show me the lists, and they show that Mr. Leclair was unfairly treated compared to the other students."

Humphrey looks at Vassago with murderous intent as his fists squeeze at his sides.

"Now, Mr. Humphrey, what do you think are our options if the latter is determined? One, you could rectify the situation immediately by deducting a detention from Mr. Leclair's current count, or two, you could maintain it. Maintaining it only will incur additional costs in legal fees and time spent in court when we sue you. Though, please do feel free to take that route; I always have particularly loved seeing court rulings in my favor."

*Holy fuck, he's good.*

Judging by the vein in Green's forehead that looks like it's about to burst, he just might be too good.

Green sighs, typing something into his computer. "Here."

He twists the laptop toward Vassago, who leans forward, scrolling down before reaching over to grab the mouse, and clicking a couple of times.

"Wonderful. He was sent the email and text separately from the others, and mere minutes before mandatory prayer." My blood suddenly runs cold as Vassago goes quiet, turning to look at Humphrey whose complexion matches that of a cherry tomato.

"That's impossible."

Vassago looks between the principal and Mr. Green with his eyebrow raised. "Is it?" As if to emphasize his point, he reaches over to the edge of the laptop, turning it to Humphrey. "See for yourself, then."

Vassago crosses his arms as Humphrey leans forward, muttering a curse under his breath before turning to Mr. Green. "What the hell is going on, Green?"

The teacher's eyes widen in disbelief before flicking to the rest of us, and something in me screams that he didn't expect Humphrey to suddenly turn on him. He stammers out incoherent words as Humphrey slams his fists onto the table.

I flinch at the sudden noise, and my pulse skyrockets as I fight to not react to the aggression. Vassago's eyes flick to me, but I stay focused on the obvious threat in the room, standing mere feet from me.

"Well, Humphrey, which option will you decide to take?" Vassago's rich voice feels like a safety net, or a bulletproof shield to stand behind as I hold on to it with every part of me.

"The detention doesn't stand and will be deducted. Mr. Leclair will remain at two until the day comes where he is found at fault for unruliness."

My heart soars in satisfaction, and my attention flicks to Vassago, only to find his eyes already locked onto mine. His lips twitch slightly before he turns to the others.

"Wonderful. I'm so glad we were able to sort this out without messy legalities. Here is my card. I'd recommend holding onto it." He places his business card into Humphrey's hand before he turns toward me and walks toward the door. His hand returns to the small of my back as he pauses, tilting his head over his shoulder. "I'll be expecting all copies of those records to be emailed to me by this afternoon, along with the waiver signed by Mr. Leclair on his first day. You should already have the request for production of documents in your inbox, Mr. Humphrey."

He guides me out of the classroom, and I'm in a daze until we're down the hall.

"Are you alright?"

I turn to look behind us, seeing no one within earshot before looking at him with wide eyes. "How did you do that?"

He chuckles, holding the door to the parking lot open. "I've been doing this for a while, and I had a hunch based on what you said that there was more to the story that we were not aware of."

I huff a quiet laugh, but it comes out as more of a scoff. "That's a large gamble to make based off a hunch. What if the computer showed everything was sent correctly?"

Vassago just shrugs, pausing to look at the dark clouds above us. "I never seriously considered it wouldn't."

My jaw drops, and I gape at him. "How the hell did you get here so fast, anyway?"

He grins at me, like I should know the answer to that. "What do you think I do for a living, Azura? I was already heading here to interview Anna. Thankfully, I finished early and heard a commotion from the office before I left."

My cheeks suddenly burn hot. "Oh."

"Now..." He turns, his gaze sliding down to mine with unexpected seriousness. "Are you going to tell me why you were crying earlier?"

I blink once, twice, three times before my mouth opens and snaps shut.

*Does the man have a memory of an elephant?*

"Azura."

I swallow.

Growing up as the older sibling in a house where the protector was the source of pain and suffering meant being the strong one. It meant putting my feelings aside and caring for others.

What was going on in my mind, or body, meant nothing so long as Cole wasn't in pain. Even when we escaped with mom, she never stopped to ask me anything as we slowly healed and moved on from that madness.

But to have someone I hardly know, ask this...

His light grey eyes search my face patiently, as if he can see the inner turmoil churning inside my mind like waves slamming against the thick barriers I've erected to protect myself from the onslaught of emotions I'd repressed.

"I—" My mouth goes dry, and my heart feels like it's going to crawl out of my throat. "We went to see our mom today, and she's awake, but she might as well be unconscious." The words coming out of my mouth feel like they're an assault on my own ears. As if they shouldn't be spoken aloud at all. "Cole has been through enough. He doesn't deserve to watch her deteriorate into nothing."

There's a long moment of silence as Vassago searches my face. "And what about you?"

My chest tightens, and I shake my head. "I'm fine."

The look he's giving me tells me he doesn't believe a word of it, but he doesn't push me any further as he glances at the parking lot. A moment of silence passes as the concrete beyond the portico darkens from the rain that's drizzling from the sky.

"Sometimes, to properly care for those we love most, we must first care for ourselves, Azura."

His eyes find mine again, and I nod. "I hear you."

There's a long moment of silence between us before a hint of amusement paints his features. "Do you?"

I go to respond, but my mouth snaps shut as I consider his question more, and after a few drawn out seconds of him giving me a knowing grin, I sigh.

"Unfortunately, I do."

His smile widens, and the rain cloud finally gives way to the sun as his expression turns thoughtful. "Would you like to go get coffee?"

Something in the way he asks has my stomach doing somersaults, and I nod.

"Sure. I'd like that."

# Chapter 11

We pull into the parking lot of a nearby café, and butterflies soar through my body.

It has taken all my willpower to keep myself from thinking this is anything more than just an attorney and client getting coffee with one another. The moment my imagination suggested otherwise, I shoved those thoughts away with force.

Vassago is a successful, well-established attorney with his own practice. His concern for me is merely to ensure his client is stable and not a liability to his career.

*And it's not like I'm interested in him or anything.*

Sure, he might be tall, well-dressed, and most likely extremely muscular—memories of the way his sleeves tightened around his biceps, how his pants hugged him perfectly in far too many places and the way his shirt tapered to his pants all flick through my mind before I shake my head—Okay, the guy clearly works out.

Either way, clearly he's got a lot going for him, and I'm delusional if I think this is anything more than just getting coffee.

The ghost of his hand at the small of my back finds its way into the forefront of my mind, and I sigh.

*Yep. Delusional.*

Pulling the car into a parking spot, I exhale a steadying breath before grabbing my purse and getting out of the car.

*Here goes nothing.*

I take six steps before my gaze lands on Vassago as he waits for me halfway between my car and the café with his hands in his pockets. His knuckles make indents in the material, and I'm keenly aware of the way his pants hug his thighs, or how his tattooed chest shows ever so slightly from where the top button is undone on his shirt.

*Just coffee, Az. Get it together.*

"Do you come here often?" No sooner have the words left my mouth than I'm cringing at my question. Thankfully, Vassago seems oblivious, or he's blissfully not reacting as he smiles warmly.

"I do not, so they'll either sink or swim. Their seating area looks nice, though." He muses, tilting his head to point to the series of couches and chairs with coffee tables for outside seating.

My eyebrows shoot up. "That's not half bad, actually."

As I'm nearing the door, Vassago takes long strides forward, opening it before his other hand outstretches toward me.

I instinctively brace myself, feeling my heart stutter as the hand that was outstretched finds its way to the small of my back again.

*It's just a nice gesture. Don't overthink it, Az.*

By the time we've ordered our drinks and sat down outside, my body is warm and my heart feels like it's trying to beat its way out of my chest.

It doesn't help that after I sat down on a mid-sized couch, Vassago took the seat directly beside me, giving minimal space because of the sheer size of him.

He takes a sip of his coffee, and I go to do the same but wince when it's too hot to drink yet.

"So, what else do we need to do before filing this case?" Part of me feels silly because my question makes it seem like I know nothing about the legal system or how it progresses.

To his credit, Vassago just grins. "We're close. Once they produce documents, we'll nearly have everything we need."

He takes another sip of his drink before placing it on the table, and I track the movements as he leans back onto one shoulder, angling himself toward me as he relaxes.

There's not much more I can do than nod. "Great." My voice comes out breathless and somehow that only makes him smile more.

My stomach does somersaults again as he chuckles. "Considering the amount of evidence and witness accounts, there's already a solid case here. That's not to mention that you have me at your side."

*Confidence is never a bad thing, right?*

I nod. "That's good, right? That means that this will be over soon."

He winces, and I glance at the way he thumbs the lip of his drink. "I can't be certain at this point. There are too many variables and unknowns for me to see the result. I can tell you that most paths seem to lead to us winning, though I won't lie and say it won't be hard fought."

Taking a cautious sip of my coffee, I gently set it down alongside his. "I see..."

"You know," he tilts his head to the side curiously. "I've had a handful of cases as of recent where organizations had... a little too much zeal with their business, but I have to say, to require mandatory prayer or face expulsion, well, it seems rather harsh."

I huff a dry laugh. "Honestly. I bet they didn't think they'd get caught, though. I mean, we live in the middle of nowhere, so it's not like there's a lot of eyes on them." Feeling Vassago's attention on me, I shrug. "They probably thought they were safe to do whatever they wanted."

He hums in agreement, taking another sip before murmuring into the lid. "So much for that. Little did they know Azura Leclair's watchful eye was on them."

My eyes widen as they lock onto his, and humor paints his features. "I wouldn't have even known had they not given my brother detention."

He just grins before his face turns contemplative. "Still, it is rather bold of them to outwardly display something that breaches a fundamental part of this country."

I nod, following his line of thought. "Makes you wonder if they did so because they have no resistance from any other entities or companies."

"Doesn't it?" His eyes linger on me, and I can't help but feel satisfied by the knowing look he gives me. It's like he's following my train of thought the same way I'm following his. As if we're both looking for the motive behind why they're so openly forceful with their practice.

Is this why he was so quick to take this case? Maybe he suspects I'm suffocating under Blackwell, and I'd do well under him instead.

My cheeks warm.

The wordless agreement in his expression only serves to reaffirm my delusion, and another swirl of butterflies churns inside my core.

A horn blares down the street, and I take another sip of my drink. "So how long have you had your own law firm?"

There's a mischievous glimmer in his light grey eyes as he grins. "Ah, far too long to count. I'm afraid I may age myself too much if I admit to that, and I'd rather not have that kind of existential crisis on a good day like this."

I huff a small laugh. "Fair. I won't rain on your parade, but I have to say your building is impressive. What made you decide to pursue law?"

I'm overly aware that my questions are merely skin deep, but there's a part of me that feels viciously curious to learn more about him, so I opt to keep him talking.

Vassago watches a car pass by on the street. "When I was younger, I found myself in a bit of a mess. You see, my brothers and I are part of a rather large family, and, as families tend to, we had one hell of a falling out. Not long after, I was stuck in what felt like limbo as many of us were, without a purpose or motivation."

Our eyes meet, and he takes another sip before he continues. "To exist without a purpose is akin to madness, Azura. At least, for me it is, and the longer I spent learning about the world around me, the more flawed it seemed. With each inconsistency, each crack in the foundation, I grew impatient and rebelled against injustice for my brothers, or those I'd grown to care about. But, it wasn't until I'd discovered how truly corrupt the justice system can be that I'd decided to pursue a career in law."

I watch as he absently thumbs the rim of his lid again. "Humans are susceptible to influence, perhaps more than either of us really know. Because of this, corruption has a seed to take root, and even if there are hundreds of people screaming for change, usually those in power are the ones who really control it. So, it would seem that even my passion to seek justice for those who deserve it would be an uphill battle."

The way he talks is like he's struggled to win cases, and I feel a pit form in my stomach. "So is there little hope then for us?"

My voice comes out more quiet and tentative than intended, and he shakes his head with a grin. "Oh, quite the opposite. I'm wholly confident that so long as we tread cautiously, we will win. You **do** have the best attorney in the state representing you."

There's a long moment of silence, and my curiosity rears its head at the thought of his history. "Did your family ever recover from the falling out?"

He winces. "No. Not exactly. We're still split. My eldest brother is–" Vassago's lips purse before twitching with barely restrained humor. "–Well, he's currently in the midst of uncovering the root cause of this whole falling out to begin with. So, until he's ready, all we can do is wait."

I take another sip and frown. "He's doing that all by himself? He didn't want help?"

Vassago just shrugs. "He has some help, but we have such a large family and the misfeasance runs deep. Bringing too many into it would only risk further dismantling of our family."

I nod, still trying to absorb all the information he's given and what that means when his phone rings.

He hardly glances at the screen before bringing it to his ear. "My dearest Ori. What—" His face turns serious as his brows pinch together. "Well, isn't that an interesting development. Did he say when?"

In an effort to not eavesdrop more than necessary, I watch a woman bringing her child inside the café before I look at the white SUV parked down the road, noticing its windows that are tinted so dark that it's impossible to see inside.

I'm still absently looking at the scenery around us as Vassago ends the call and slides his phone into his pocket. "My sincerest apologies, Azura."

My cheeks burn at the formality mixed with the flutter in my body as he says my name. "Just call me Az, please."

He inclines his head slightly with a smile. "So, how is your brother holding up?"

A twinge of guilt churns in my stomach as I consider that Cole is being picked up by Elena this afternoon instead of me, all so that I can have coffee with Vassago. "He's struggling. Probably more than even I'm aware of. He's always been quiet, you know?"

My gaze slides to Vassago, and I can see the question written in his face as I resign myself to allowing him the smallest insight into our past.

"Our father was not kind. He drank too much, took advantage of his power over us, and mom didn't realize it until it was almost too late." My eyes remain glued to the street as I continue on. "By the time we escaped him, Cole had already endured far more than any ten-year-old should."

When I glance over, Vassago's light grey eyes feel like they can see directly into my soul as he searches my face with a soft expression. "And how old were you when the abuse started?"

A twist of dread settles like a bag of rocks in my stomach, and my teeth clench as my mind fights to disassociate myself from the memories. "Too young."

The muscle in his jaw feathers, but he holds my gaze. "You said you escaped him. He's alive?"

I chew my cheek. "Maybe? We left after mom gave him sleeping pills when he was drunk." The realization that I may have just incriminated myself for knowing or mom for possibly killing him hits me, and my eyes widen as my hand shoots to cover my mouth.

Vassago looks at me with a mixture of confusion and concern. "What is it?"

His expression is genuine, and it hardly takes more than a second for it to turn into understanding as he laughs under his breath. "You really think I'd go after your mother for drugging him?"

Blinking, my mouth drops open before snapping shut.

*Do I?*

His grin widens, and I shake my head. "I'd hope not, but admittedly, I don't really know you all that well."

He considers me for a moment before tilting his head, and the setting sun shines into his eyes, making them look like thousands of dazzling shards of grey ice.

"That's fair. Well, even if she'd murdered him, whoever he is, he deserved it for abusing his own children. If anything, she should have poisoned him, slowly... but only after making sure he had a fabulous life insurance policy."

My jaw drops. "Are you sure you're an attorney?"

His brows shoot up and humor paints his features. "Did I say that was legal advice? That was purely wishful thinking."

We both laugh, and I go to take another sip of my coffee.

There's a long moment of comfortable silence before he rests his coffee on his knee. "I assume he is the reason you flinched in Humphrey's office?"

I can feel his gaze lingering on me as I nod. "It's either fight or flight, you know?" My voice drops low, and I consider how far I've come in the four years since we escaped him. "It used to be worse. Footsteps in the hallway used to trigger me, car doors shutting outside."

"Did you ever consider killing him?"

My eyes widen, and I'm about to argue it's wrong, but I can't.

Not when the memory of running at him with a kitchen knife is seared into my brain.

"The first time I caught him with Cole, I tried." His jaw tenses, and I don't know if it's my admission or the subject. "I'd come home early and heard something from Cole's room. It took me all of ten seconds to run to the kitchen and grab the knife off the counter. By the time I was in the room and buried it into his shoulder, I realized that would not stop him. I'd pulled it out, and tried to go for his face, but, I'd only injured him."

I look over at Vassago, and I'm fully prepared for him to think less of me as my pulse rages in my ears. "I paid the price for it in the end, but I nearly became a murderer that night."

"Not all murders are the same, Az." He whispers, and my heart tumbles. "You were brave to do what you did."

Desperate to lighten the mood, I huff a dry laugh. "Are you saying you condone violence, sir?"

I'm fully intending for my emphasis on the last word to sound more teasing, but the way heat flashes across his expression sends my pulse into overdrive.

"Violence, sometimes, is the only answer." He pauses. "That's not legal advice, of course."

Desperate to do something with my hands, I go to take another sip of my drink. The base tilts up way too easily, and I freeze when it's upside down with nothing coming out.

He must notice as he chuckles more. "Should we have gotten a larger size?" Pulling out his phone, I glance at his screen as he checks the time and my brows shoot up.

*It's been two and a half hours already?*

It feels like we just got started talking, and I know I don't want this to end. "Time flies when we're having fun, I guess."

*Cringe-worthy.*

Vassago just nods in agreement, reaching over to grab my drink before throwing both cups out in the garbage beside him. "I suppose I should get back. My brother and his wife will be terribly upset if I don't make it home soon."

"You live with them?"

The question comes out before I can give a second thought, and I'm kicking myself when he just nods.

"My brother and I are close. We've been through a lot, and when our family split, we knew we could rely on one another for every-thing. He dragged me into his organized chaos when he met his wife–who is wonderful, by all means–and we just never changed our living arrangement."

My vicious curiosity rears its head. "What does he do for work?"

Vassago pushes to his feet, offering a hand toward me with his palm open. "He's been a professor at Divine Covenant College for a few years now."

My brows shoot up, and I slide my hand into his palm automati-cally, ignoring the way nervous butterflies soar through my body.

At this point, I don't know if I crave his touch, or I'm afraid of it, but my lack of any outward reaction tells me there's a good chance it's not the latter.

I don't even want to think about what that might mean for me after a lifetime of being averse to touch from nearly everyone.

"What does he teach?"

"Religious studies."

I blink, and he helps me to my feet before leading the way to the parking lot. "Is your family religious?"

His lips twitch upwards at the corners with suppressed amusement. "In some senses of the word."

Not wanting to push further, I opt to change the topic slightly. "And his wife? What does she do?"

By the time we're near my car, he pauses, putting his hands in his pockets with a gentle smile. "She's a counselor, though one may argue she's also a full-time babysitter for my brother."

The laugh that escapes me is genuine, and I see his own smile widen in response, sending a rush of dopamine through me.

He glances around, his gaze lingering down the street before pinning me in place at the driver's side door. "Thank you for this. I'll be in touch once these final interviews are done, and we can discuss our next steps."

My heart feels like it's in my throat as I nod. "This was fun."

"Drive safe, Az." He waves his hand over his head as he turns to walk to his car, and I cast a lingering glance in his direction before hurrying into the driver's side.

An emotion I'm not willing to process tightens my chest as I buckle myself in. When his engine roars beside me, I slide my key in the ignition before fiddling with the radio.

It was refreshing to meet someone so down to earth and open, even if he's my attorney.

*Can you even become intimately involved with your lawyer?*

*Doesn't that bring some level of conflict of interest?*

I suddenly realize my line of thought and blink rapidly before putting the car into drive.

*Nope.*

*No more of that.*

Those kinds of thoughts will get me in trouble... If I'm not already, at this point.

# Chapter 12

It's only been three days since I got coffee with Vassago, and I think I might be losing my mind.

Not because of anything to do with the case but because he's been stuck in my mind so much that I'm near certain I should charge him rent.

In fact, I've replayed our time at the café over so many times in my head that I've been almost positive that my delusion has imagined his mustang in Blackwell's parking lot, parked on the street near the house and at Cole's school when I drop him off.

And as I climb out of the car to go into the grocery store, I'm watching the grey vehicle pulling into the lot with a note of nervous excitement.

Could it be him?

When I chance a look over, my heart sinks when it's not the right make of vehicle.

My heart slides into my stomach. *I really need to get it together.*

I turn forward to head in the doors as they slide open, and collide with a hard body.

"Oh, Jesus." I gasp, feeling something crushed between me and the stranger before it drops to the ground. My eyes are wide as I look at the chocolate cake that's splattered on the ground, and horror washes over me at the white icing that's splattered onto an expensive looking suit.

It's not until my line of vision drags up to see Vassago's expression mirroring the shock my own that my tummy tumbles.

"I'm most definitely not." His lips twitch upward, but I'm still horrified that I've not only destroyed his cake but also managed to ruin his pants as he chuckles.

"Vassago, I–" At a loss for words, I gesture to the cake before covering my face with my hands. "Oh my god. I wasn't paying attention, I'm so sorry."

When I look at him, he just shakes his head with barely restrained amusement, and a worker steps over. "I can clean this up."

The kid looks no older than fifteen, and he kneels down with a bag to shovel pieces of the cake in. Vassago side steps, and I spot the dollop of icing on his shoe with a wave of guilt.

"Hold on–" I say, and he freezes as I grab the paper towels from beside the worker, ripping a couple off. Within seconds I'm kneeling in front of Vassago, wiping the icing off the tip of his shoe before throwing the towel into the bag that now holds the destroyed cake.

Before pushing to my feet I look up, only to find his head tilted to the side as he watches me. Our eyes meet, and my heart stutters when he offers his hand between us. His fingertips just barely brush against my jaw, and it takes a conscious effort to continue to breathe as I slide my palm into his.

"I'll pay for–"

"Not a chance in Hell." He interrupts as he pulls me to my feet, and someone passes by us to enter the grocery store as I shake my head. Internally I'm arguing that I ruined his pants **and** his cake as he watches the worker scurry inside.

"If you don't let me pay for another one, I'll just find another way to pay you back."

He looks at me thoughtfully. "How about this, since that was their last black forest cake, and this was the only place I could find for miles that made them; if you can find another one, we will call it even."

I blink at him, and my heart flutters in my chest. "Okay, I think I can help with that."

Turning to the parking lot, when he doesn't follow me, I pause. He's still by the doors, and he gestures inside. "Were you not here to get something?"

I glance inside, weighing how bad I need the milk and carrots before sighing. "Are you okay to wait a couple minutes?"

He just grins. "I have all the time in the world, Az."

I'm pulling in to Elena's bakery with my groceries tucked into the passenger seat, glancing at Vassago's mustang in my rearview every few seconds as if this was all some kind of fever dream.

But he doesn't disappear.

His sleek, dark vehicle pulls up alongside mine, and I cut off the engine before I gathering my things into my purse. When I turn to the door, it clicks and swings open.

The way he steps aside and holds it in place has my delusion coming full circle, and I climb out of the driver's seat, passing by him with a murmur of thanks.

"Do you prefer the desserts from this bakery?" He inquires, his grey irises surveying the front window.

"My mom's friend, she lives next door and owns this place." I say, taking the steps up to the door. "We don't get to come here often but she usually brings cakes over for our birthdays. They're really good."

The door chimes as we walk inside, and I hear something clatter from the back before Elena's blonde hair comes into view as she turns the corner. Her white apron is covered with flour and icing as she smiles warmly.

"Azura, it's so good to see you." Her eyes land on Vassago, and she blinks as she glances between us. "Oh, I'm sorry I don't think we've met. You are...?"

Vassago tall form leans in and shakes her hand gently. "Vassago, I'm a friend of Azura's."

My body warms.

"Oh. Well, any friend of Azura's is a friend of mine!" She chimes. "So, what can I do for you two?"

"Actually, I was hoping maybe you had a black forest cake?"

She looks at me thoughtfully before her eyebrows shoot up. "Yes!"

She hurries into the back, and a fridge door opening fills the air before slamming shut, and her quick footsteps draw near as she turns the corner. "Here!"

Sliding it onto the table, I'm pulling out my wallet when she waves her hands dismissively between us. "Nuh, uh, uh. Family doesn't pay!"

"Thank you, Elena." I murmur and she just smiles, but the sadness behind it makes my heart squeeze.

Elena may not be our blood relative, but she's been kind to us since we moved here that she might as well be family. She slides the cake over to me, and I turn to Vassago as he reaches over to shake her hand gently.

Before I can get to the door, he reaches around me for the doorknob, twisting and holding it open. His abdomen brushes my arm before my shoulder, and I swallow as I head to the car.

My gaze drops to the beautifully designed cake, cherries atop dollops of icing with chocolate shavings lining the side, and my heart sinks when I consider who this could be for.

I'm painfully aware that I'm hurting my own feelings by assuming he's taken. There's no way he's not.

"Is the cake for a special someone?" I ask, unable to stop myself and I cringe. *Smooth. Real smooth.*

He's blissfully unaware or oblivious to my struggles as he huffs a laugh. "If by special someone you mean the child my brother has been fostering, then yes."

My cheeks burn, and a guilty wave of relief washes over me. "That's sweet of you to pick it up for him."

I walk the cake to his passenger door, cursing myself for not giving him more room when I parked. There's hardly enough space for me to walk between the sides of our vehicles. When I get close to the passenger door, I feel his hand at my waist and freeze.

The contact makes my chest feel light while my core flips chaotically, and it only worsens when he leans over my shoulder for the handle. He's so close that his woodsy cologne invades my senses, and it takes a conscious effort to not inhale a deep lungful.

God, he smells good.

His hand on my waist disappears as he opens the door, swapping hands to hold it open, and I lean in to place it securely in the seat.

Straightening, I turn, only to come chest to chest with Vassago, and my pulse that was already beating hard nearly trips over itself as my heart rate spikes.

"You're quite the savior for having a friend as a baker, Az." He murmurs with a soft expression. "Thank you."

My head tilts up, and my breath gets caught in my lungs as he brushes a stray lock of hair from my face. My chest rises and falls hard as his fingertips brush the shell of my ear.

"You wouldn't have needed a savior if I hadn't ruined your first cake. I hope your foster nephew likes it."

Though, some small part of me is thankful to have gotten to see him. Not that I'll admit to that out loud.

He smiles, stepping aside to shut the passenger door. "Vince will love it. I'm certain if he knew it was from you, he'd love it even more."

My heart squeezes as he opens my driver's side door, and I climb inside as he leans down slightly to look at me.

"Drive safe, Az."

# Chapter 13

*Four days later*

"Mrs. Merrick?"

She hardly bothers looking up from her phone as she stands from her chair in the waiting room, and her heels click rhythmically toward the now open door to Blackwell's office.

My phone buzzes at my desk, and the moment she breezes past me, I hurry over to it, feeling a nervous excitement rifle through my limbs.

These past few days, the hospital had said mom was getting better, and to expect an update on whether she'll be able to go home in the coming days.

With trembling fingers, I fumble as my thumb slides across the screen, and I place the phone to my ear as rhythmic beeping and voices carry from the other side of the line.

"Hello?" My voice wavers as I try to keep my voice quiet.

"Hi, is this Ms. Leclair?"

"Yes, this is Azura Leclair."

"Ms. Leclair, this is Tiffany Fornell with Providence Medical Institute. Are you available to speak for a moment?"

My heart rate spikes, and I glance at the closed door to Blackwell's office. "Uh, yes. I can."

"Ms. Leclair, there's no easy way to tell you this." A wave of dread washes over me, and I freeze in place. "Your mom's been moved back to intensive care after she suffered a stroke. We have her stable for now, but wanted to see if you could come in and complete some paperwork and speak with the doctor."

Feeling leaves my body, and goosebumps break out over my skin as a shiver wracks through me.

"Yeah," I whisper, nodding even though she can't see me. "I'll be there in thirty." My hands fumble under the desk for the strap of my purse, before I'm hurrying out the door.

It's as if I'm on autopilot, dazed and half aware of my surroundings as I slide into the driver's seat and turn on the engine. The rumble fills the air around me, and it's almost suffocating.

*She was doing better.*

*We thought she'd be coming home soon.*

*How could this have happened?*

I'm halfway to the hospital when my phone buzzes loudly, and I nearly jump out of my own skin at the sound before reaching over to press my thumb against the green button on the screen.

"Hello?" I hardly recognize my own voice.

"Azura? Where the hell are you?"

*Shit.*

"Uh, sorry, Mr. Blackwell. The hospital called. My mom has an emergency and I'm headed to the hospital. I'm s—"

The vehicle in front of me brakes hard, and I slam my foot to the floor as my car lurches to a stop.

Blackwell scoffs. "Unbelievable."

"Mr. Blackwell, I—"

"We'll talk when you're back in the office, Ms. Leclair."

The line abruptly disconnects, and in any normal circumstance I'd be panicking about his perception, about the ramifications of my absence or lack of communication, but all I feel right now is numb.

Blowing out a breath, I ease on the gas again, feeling the tremble in my arms from frayed nerves as the car approaches an intersection up ahead.

It's like a blanket of ice has washed over my being, keeping everything else at bay, shielding me from the emotional chaos threatening to take control at the slightest misstep.

I know I should have told him I was leaving, but at the moment, everything else other than mom has disappeared, much like the day when I attacked Jeffrey for what he did to Cole.

My attention snaps to the present as I bring the car to a stop at the red light.

*Cole.*

Glancing at the intersection, I'm torn in indecision.

If I turn around to get him from school, I may run out of whatever little time I have to see mom. But if I don't go get him, Cole won't have a way to get home, and Elena isn't able to help when she's working.

*What should I do?*

The cross traffic comes to a stop, and the empty turn lane gets a green light, my pulse hikes up.

*If I leave Cole at school, I'm only exposing him to more risk of detention, or worse.*

The car in front of me accelerates as tears flow down my cheeks.

*But I need to get to the hospital to see the doctor before he leaves.*

My foot presses on the gas, and a mixture of guilt and anxiety churn my stomach with each second that passes.

*God, if anything happens to Cole because of this, I will never forgive myself.*

By the time the car's in the hospital parking lot, my heart's in my throat. The tears finally stopped staining my cheeks but still threaten to fall from the corners of my eyes, and I exhale a ragged breath before lifting my phone to text Cole.

*If he can hold on for an hour and not get into trouble at school, I'll be able to come get him after.*

After dialing the PIN, the screen unlocks just as another call comes in, and I see Vassago's name on the caller ID. I stare at it for a long moment before pressing the button to answer, feeling my throat constrict from the ball of emotions in it.

"Hello?" My voice comes out as more of a croak, and my lips thin.

"Az?"

I inhale and my breath hitches. "What is it, Vassago?"

There's a long moment of silence before his level voice fills the air. "I wanted to connect about the indictment, but... that can wait. What's wrong?"

A rogue tear streams down my cheek, and I shake my head. "It's nothing."

"Az..." Vassago's voice is soft but warning before he continues. "You can either tell me, or I'll find out for myself."

I swallow hard, my gaze flicking to a white SUV as it leaves the hospital parking lot.

"Vassago, I—"

"Spill it."

Blowing out a breath, I lean back into the seat. "The hospital called me to see mom. She had a stroke. I need to see the doctor before he leaves, and Cole is stuck at school."

There's a moment of silence, and I pull my purse into my lap before getting out of the car.

"How far are you from the hospital?"

I glance at the entrance. "Roughly twenty feet away."

"I'll pick up your brother from school. Providence Medical, right?"

My jaw drops. "I–" My voice cuts off before I can argue, knowing full well that I'm not in a place to decline his help. "Are you sure?"

Vassago's quiet chuckle sounds out, but his tone drops low. "I wouldn't have said so if I wasn't certain. I'm already in the area. I'll pick him up."

Relief washes over me, and tears spring to my eyes as I take in a deep breath. "Thank you, Vassago."

"See you soon, Az." His voice is strangely soft before the line disconnects, and I hurry into the hospital.

# Chapter 14

Each step down the linoleum hallway feels more imposing, and by the time I'm outside of the double set doors to intensive care, with a rhythmic beeping sounding out from each room around me, my heart feels like it could rattle out of my chest.

"Ms. Leclair?"

I twist to see Dr. Harper standing behind me with a clipboard in his arm, and brimming anxiety makes my fingers tremble.

"Dr. Harper, good to see you."

He gives me a tight smile. "I'm glad you could come on such short notice. It's been touch and go for the past few hours."

Swallowing, I nod. "How is she?"

He searches my face for a moment before releasing a sigh. "She had a clot in the carotid artery in her neck, which caused an ischemic stroke. She displayed evidence of paralysis when the nurse was in to administer her medications. Thankfully, the nurse identified it quickly, but because of her condition since arriving here, she'll have to remain admitted until further notice."

Crossing my arms over my chest, I nod. "I understand. Is she awake?"

He shakes his head, glancing past me as if he can see through the doors and all the way to her room. "Not yet. She's currently receiving medications intravenously to treat the clot, so we're hoping to see some recovery over the next twenty-four hours." Dr. Harper offers the clipboard between us tentatively. "Considering that her prognosis is still unknown, we will need to have you review this paperwork as her power of attorney and next of kin."

I glance down to see a list of steps to take when caring for someone in their final stages of life.

*This can't be real.*

"Can I go see her?" My voice sounds awfully quiet, and he nods, gesturing toward the door.

"Please."

Not bothering to look at him any longer, I turn in the opposite direction and push through the doors, seeing a panel on the wall with "Leclair" on it before I walk inside.

Seeing the strong, resilient woman I thought would live forever in this state is beyond shocking.

She looks like she's lost weight since we last visited. The bones in her wrists are more pronounced, her already fair skin has turned near translucent in areas, and half her face looks more droopy than the other. Her greasy hair looks like it's been recently brushed, and my heart squeezes knowing that the nurses would take the time to do such a small thing when caring for her.

The tubes and wires attached to her look like something out of a movie.

I stare at her for a long moment, thinking back to the day when Jeffrey had gone out of town for work, and she'd taken us to the movie theater for the first time.

The only movie we were in time for was a sci-fi horror that was–looking back–wildly inappropriate for any kids to be watching, but the scene where the heroine wakes up in deep space with a million connections attached to her, keeping her alive, is a stark similarity.

I pace to the side of the bed, picking up the nearest chair and setting it alongside her.

My chest squeezes as I slide my hand into hers, feeling how lightweight and limp it is against my palm.

*She was supposed to get through this.*

*We didn't escape Jeffrey just for fucking cancer to steal her away.*

Tears spring to my eyes, and I remember each time she'd come home from her double shifts with Jeffrey already fast asleep on the couch.

After she knew what he had been doing to us, she'd knock at my door and slip into bed with me as I'd sob.

*She never asked, but I think she knew.*

*She knew, but she was powerless to get us out.*

*"Take care of your brother."*

*"Don't let Cole out of your sight."*

*"Some day it'll just be the two of you."*

*"Be strong for me, Azura."*

*"Be strong."*

Who knew that years later, those would be the words that would stick with me.

A rogue tear slips down my cheek, and the floodgates open as another drops to the bed.

*I wish it didn't have to be this way. I wish evil people like Jeffrey would be the target of disease, not people like mom, fighting every day to get by.*

*Why is this so unfair?*

A sob crawls out of my throat, and I press my forehead to the bed. My body trembles with each hitch of my breath, and I'm once again reminded of what faith has brought to us.

Because if there was a God out there, Jeffrey would be the one laying cold and alone, living out his last days in a hospital bed, and mom would be fine.

Instead, this woman who gave her entire adult life to providing for us, will have her life cut short.

And I'll be the one to pick up the mantle, because that's how it's always been, hasn't it?

I'm not ready to raise Cole by myself, though. I'm hardly years into my own adulthood as a woman, let alone becoming a surrogate mother.

Is that my purpose here? To suffer and become the mother of the house. To sacrifice a life of my own so that Cole can have his?

A wave of frustration builds inside of me, and I shake my head against the sheets of the hospital bed.

Everything I've done has been for Cole. Everything mom did was for us. We live a life doing deeds for others, yet tragedy finds us every god, damn, time.

I lift my head, looking at the strongest woman I know through blurred vision, and tears trail down my cheeks. They pool at my chin and drop to my lap in a steady stream.

Some day when I die, in the infinitesimal chance I wind up before those pearly gates... I don't know that I'd walk through them.

Because to do so would be to accept that there was no other option for mom.

That this was the only way it could have gone.

That this step forward without her had to happen, and I'm just not ready or willing to accept it.

Resting my head against the sheets again, my mind spirals and I squeeze my eyes shut at the frustration and despair clouding my thoughts.

I don't know how long it takes for my mind to clear, but by the time it does, sleep claims me.

# Chapter 15

A quiet creak jolts me awake, and I jerk upright to see Cole peering through the door with tears in his eyes.

"Mom?" The sound of his voice nearly breaks me as he hurries over to her side, grasping her frail hand in his. Tears stream down his cheeks as he leans in to press a trembling kiss to her forehead, hovering above her as droplets fall onto her pale skin.

The prayers he's said every night echo in the back of my mind as my arms wrap around my body in a failed effort to soothe the ache growing in my chest.

*He hardly got to know her. Hell, I hardly got to know her too.*

*We may have had to support one another through hell, but if it wasn't for her, we'd still be there.*

Cole turns away slightly, obscuring my line of sight to his face and I take that as my cue to give him privacy.

Turning to the door, my gaze lands on Vassago's somber expression. He says nothing as I push past the doorway, feeling his presence at my back as he follows me out.

Each step feels like I'm weighted down until I finally come to a stop, with the image of Cole's heartbreak clear in my mind. My tears spill over, trailing down my cheeks as my eyes squeeze shut.

Vassago's footsteps fill the air to my right, and I exhale a ragged breath before opening my eyes to look at him. The light grey of his irises is exceptionally bright against the fluorescent lights, and the knowing look he gives me only tightens my chest even more.

He searches my face for a moment before his gaze drops to my arms, still wrapped tight around my body. A flicker of emotion graces his features, and his arms move to encircle my shoulders, but he freezes when I stiffen.

My mind screams that it wants this, and my heart echoes the sentiment, but my body is at war with both as understanding flashes across his face.

"I should have asked—" He goes to withdraw his arms and I shake my head, quickly interrupting him.

"Wait." My hushed voice trembles. "Please."

He pauses, and I unravel my arms, taking a deep breath as I step in close, feeling his chest against mine. Wrapping my arms around his body, my movements are cautious, and stiff as I fight the urge to withdraw into myself.

With my palms splayed over his back, my cheek leans against his collar, and I feel his arms encircle my shoulders. He mirrors my caution before his arms tighten, and a shudder wracks through my body before a wave of relief follows it.

I'm surrounded by what feels like the closest thing to safety, and it makes me swallow hard against the lump in my throat.

Years and years of aversion to touch from anyone but Cole, while still craving physical interaction, made me dread this moment.

For so long, I'd experienced anxiety, terror, discomfort, and fear when people would so much as put their arm around me. To go this long, wondering if I'd ever enjoy physical touch, only for Vassago to be the one person who doesn't trigger a negative reaction...

His chin rests against the top of my head as his arms tighten. "Az, you're shaking."

I melt into him and nod against his chest, feeling more tears spill out as the sound of his heartbeat soothes the remnants of anxiety in my mind.

"Are you sure this is okay?"

I don't know if he's asking because of my visible aversion to touch coupled with my shaking, or if he's asking because he's my attorney, but I nod again anyway.

For whatever reason, Vassago is the exception to the rule, and I couldn't be more thankful for it.

My heart stutters as his thumb soothingly glides along my arm before he rests his cheek against my hair.

Our embrace feels more intimate than any hug between two platonic friends should, but I can't seem to bring myself to care. Not when I don't know when I'll feel this...

This...

Safe.

My arms tighten around him as my tears slow to a stop, and it's a long moment before I reluctantly pull away. The moment his hands move to grip my arms in support, I mourn the absence of having him close.

"I needed that. I think more than I realized."

He searches my face for a long moment before his thumb grazes my cheek, catching the rogue tear before giving me a soft smile.

With the distance between us, and the way he's cupping my cheek, if anyone were to see us embraced like this, they'd think we were much more than just friends.

The thought sends a wave of emotion through me that I'm not ready to process just yet.

Tucking a lock of my hair behind my ear, his lips twitch. "I trust that you'll take full advantage of having my number any time you need that, then."

My heart nearly stops in my chest as he fails to suppress a slight smile before releasing me fully, glancing at the door where Cole is with mom.

"Will you two be spending the night here?"

I nod. "Dr. Harper said because of the situation and how touch and go it is, we can. There's a second unused bed that Cole can sleep on and I'll take the chair."

The sound of footsteps and a thud fills the air, and I can already picture Cole flopping into the chair with more force than necessary.

"I should go make sure he's okay."

Something inside of me twists painfully, and it only gets worse when Vassago nods, with understanding painted across his features.

"Right. I have a few things to take care of, but text me if you need."

The silence between us is maddening, and it's all I can do to nod. "Thank you, Vassago. For everything."

His expression softens, and he turns to leave down the hallway as each step makes the ache in my chest grow. Tearing my gaze from him, I slip back into the room quietly, seeing Cole with his head in his palms on the chair beside mom's bed as I make my way to him.

With the way he looks, he appears as if he's aged another five years, and looks way too contemplative for a fourteen-year-old.

My heart aches for how much my little brother has been through.

I plop down on the chair beside him, looking at mom absently as my hand rubs Cole's back in a soothing manner.

"How was school?"

His head shakes. "I don't want to talk about school right now."

"Right." I whisper. "No school talk then."

There's a long moment of silence between us before Cole leans back in his seat, and his attention settles on me.

"Are you dating?"

My eyes widen, and I stare at him in disbelief as my cheeks burn. "Am I *what*?"

He huffs a dry laugh. "Answer the question, Az."

I stare at him for a moment, and my mouth snaps shut as I shake my head. "We aren't."

Even though I mean it, it doesn't sound convincing, and I can't help but wonder if it's what my heart really wants rather than what the truth might be.

"Well, I guess we'll see how long that lasts." My eyes widen and he just grins. "I might be young, but I'm not stupid or blind, Az."

I sigh deeply, leaning back in my chair. "He's got his entire life together. I doubt he'd want to involve himself in our chaos more than he already has."

Cole's elbow jabs my arm as he gives me a matter-of-fact look. "And yet, he already has."

My eyes narrow on him. "What are you saying, Cole?"

His matter-of-fact look turns into poorly restrained humor as his gaze slides to mom's bed. "I'm saying he's already in our lives more than what I think any attorney would. I'm saying that unless he's your guardian angel or something, I don't see any other reason for him to be helping us this much."

I search his face for a long moment as my mind wars between seeing his boyish features and hearing wisdom that seems far beyond his years.

"Az say something."

I feel my throat tighten. "I don't know, Cole. All I know is that I'm thankful for his help, for whatever our friendship is, and that we'd be screwed without him."

Cole hums in agreement, and slides his large hand into mine as I give it a squeeze, keeping my eyes locked onto mom's frail form on the bed.

"All I know is that whatever happens, we will still have each other."

Cole squeezes my hand back in a silent agreement, and we remain like that for a long moment.

It's hard to think of what's next when we're in crisis mode like this. Chaos overshadows every calm moment, and I can't help feeling like we're just struggling to stay afloat.

And Vassago has been the beacon in the sea of night.

Each enormous wave that I think will take us down, it's like he's been there leading us to shore.

I consider for a moment how he's literally been there for us when no one else has been, and he might actually be more like a life raft rather than a light in the dark.

"Do you think God is real, Az?"

When I look at him, his brows are furrowing ever so slightly as he focuses on mom. My mind filters through each time I'd heard him praying in his room, and I brace myself for him to finally reach the same realization that I did years ago.

I knew someday it was bound to happen.

"Why wouldn't he be?"

His hand flexes against my grip before he tilts his head back to look at the ceiling, as if trying to see into heaven itself. "Since mom got sick, I've prayed for help, for her to get better, for God to protect her."

I swallow hard against the lump forming in my throat. "And?"

A single tear trails down his cheek. "Every word I've said has been ignored."

"Have they?"

His head snaps toward me, and he frowns as he gestures toward mom. "You think this is them being answered?"

I shake my head slightly. "In the years I've observed people of faith, Cole, there's been one recurring theme that's always been there, and that's that sometimes His blessings come in ways you wouldn't expect."

"What does that even mean?"

"It means that her body is broken and there's a good chance it cannot be repaired, so what is the only other way to ease her suffering apart from what would only be considered a miracle?"

Devastation paints his features as he shakes his head in denial. "I can't handle that, Az. Why can't she just wake up, go through treatment and get better?"

The words on my tongue taste acrid as they leave my lips. "Because sometimes that's just not part of His plan."

I'm painfully aware that I don't even believe the things I'm saying, but all I can do is hope that he finds meaning behind them.

Bad things happen, and it's no one's fault. Sometimes that's just the reality we need to live with.

"Well, He has a shit plan then."

My lips twitch as I cast him a sidelong glance. "Indeed he does, little brother."

# Chapter 16

Hours have gone by with the steady beeping of mom's heart-rate monitor and various other machines nearly lulling me to sleep. My heavy eyes droop as Cole lies fast asleep on the bed next to mom's.

A soft knock at the door has my eyes flying open, and we both jolt awake as the door creaks, with Vassago's tall form peering inside.

His hair falls forward over his forehead, mussed and damp. "I hope I'm not intruding much." His eyes flick between us before he grimaces. "Ah, but I did wake you both. I apologize. Considering the circumstances, I'd assumed you wouldn't have eaten dinner, so I picked some up after finishing my errands. I hope that's okay."

My mouth drops open to answer, but before I can say anything, my stomach grumbles loudly.

"I suppose that answers that." Cole says, laughing as he sits up on the spare bed. He scoots to the edge and lets his legs dangle over as he yawns.

I watch as Vassago carries a bag to the table near the window. He unties it before walking a to-go container to where Cole sits before crossing the room and handing me a container as well.

"You really didn't have to do this, but thank you for being so com-passionate." I murmur, feeling Cole's burning gaze at the side of my head.

Vassago's expression is soft, and he glances over at mom as his jaw tenses. "We never know what moment is due to be our final, but

I think, given that she could be near hers, something tells me she wouldn't want you both starving for her sake."

My eyes find Cole chewing his burger before I take a bite myself, and Vassago walks to the door. He pauses, glancing between us. "Is there anything either of you need before I leave?"

Cole and I shake our heads, and a lump clogs my throat. "No, even just bringing us dinner was more than we could ask." My pulse hikes as I reflect on Cole's commentary earlier. "I can go home to get clothes in the morning and we can spend the day here with mom otherwise."

Vassago's expression holds a deep note of sadness that I can't seem to place as he inclines his head. "Call me if you need anything, Az."

He disappears out the door, and my chest tightens almost painfully in his absence.

*"Call me if you need anything, Az."*

My gaze widens at Cole's mocking tone, and he laughs before taking another bite of his burger.

"For a guy who is really enjoying his food, you sure have a lot of jokes about how you got it."

He just grins and pops a fry into his mouth. "I never said I wasn't grateful."

I roll my eyes and take another bite of my food as my attention turns to where mom is.

Vassago's statement from earlier really settles in as I chew.

Hopefully, we can make the most of whatever time we have left with her.

# Chapter 17

A high-pitched sound fills my ears, like the tone of a fire alarm, except it's constant. Unrelenting. The sound gets louder, and soon a repetitive thud joins it before I'm shaken awake.

"Az, wake up. It's mom!"

I jolt upright just as the door to the room opens, and two nurses hurry in. My eyes squint against the light invading my senses, blinking furiously as a rush of adrenaline floods my veins.

"Mom!" Cole's voice is quickly drowned out by the noise filling the room, and I glance around, still half disoriented from sleep.

The two nurses are hardly more than a blur as one lowers the guard rails. Their shouted words to each other sound like gibberish, and I'm struggling to comprehend them amidst the chaotic and incessant beeping as one nurse starts CPR.

That's when the events suddenly hit me, and I stare at her with wide eyes as my entire body goes cold.

She's flat-lined.

Mom's...

No...

"Mom. Mom!" My voice is shrill, and I shoot to my feet as Cole holds me in place.

The nurse not doing CPR does a double-take in our direction before walking over. "You both need to go to the hallway. Now." I move to peer over her shoulder, and she moves into my line of vision. "I need you to wait in the hallway."

Cole grips my arm, and he tugs me to the door as a doctor hurries into the room toward the bed.

"Stop!" My voice cracks as I wriggle against his frustratingly solid grip. "Cole, let me go!"

By the time we get out the door, tears are streaming down my face with the image of the nurse still doing CPR fresh in my mind.

*This can't be it. She can't be gone.*

*We still had so much to do. She was supposed to see Cole get through high school. She's going to miss him going to college. What about his first girlfriend? His first break up? When he gets married? Grandkids?*

Tears spill from my eyes as I blink my blurred vision away.

*She can't be gone.*

Cole's grip relaxes before he lets go completely, but it's only seconds that our eyes meet, and he pulls me into his trembling chest.

Or is it me that's shaking?

We remain like that for what feels like an eternity until the doors open and we break apart. My nerves are hanging on a thread as the nurse who wasn't doing CPR walks toward us.

Her slow pace, and the tentative and guarded look she wears, tells me everything I need to know as Cole shakes his head in my peripherals.

"I'm sorry–"

Cole's breath hitches, and he whirls away from us as my heart breaks all over again. He steps a few feet away, and the nurse holds my gaze as his muffled sobs fill the air.

That's when my own tears fall in earnest.

The nurse clears her throat, but the doctor from earlier steps alongside her as her mouth snaps shut. "I'm so very sorry for your loss, Ms. Leclair."

I nod, feeling numb from head to toe as the doctor prattles on about funeral arrangements, but I'm not listening to even a fraction of what he's saying as Cole sobs into his hands beside feet away.

None of this feels real.

The doctor hands me a pamphlet with information for the local funeral parlor, which only serves to heighten the odd out-of-body experience as I gingerly take it from him.

The paper feels foreign. Out of place. Unreal.

"Ms. Leclair?"

It's not until I realize that the doctor is looking at me expectantly, and I snap back into reality.

"Sorry–" I croak through the lump of emotion clogging my throat before clearing it. "Thank you. Is there anything else needed from me?"

The empathetic look the nurse gives me as she stands next to him nearly sends me back into dissociating, and the doctor shakes his head.

"No, that was everything. Do you have a relative to pick you up or to stay with?"

The thought of Jeffrey is enough to sober my numb body as my heart pounds. "No, but we will be okay. Thank you for your concern."

He frowns as if something I said confused him before glancing at the nurse. She looks like she's about to speak, but her attention flicks down the hall behind me, and her mouth snaps shut.

"Ms. Leclair." I turn to see a man taking confident strides toward us with two police officers in tow. He looks well-dressed for being in a hospital at an ungodly time of morning, and when his gaze lands on Cole, my heart nearly stops.

*No. No, she left guardianship to me in her Will. She said she did.*

He gives the nurse and doctor a tight smile before turning to me once more. "My name is Gregory Ferguson, and I'm with Child and Family Services–"

"No."

My eyes widen, and I look at Cole as his hands tighten into fists.

Ferguson looks unimpressed as he looks between us. "The City of Rennensberg requires us to bring Cole under the State's custody until the courts work through legal guardianship."

My breathing picks up as Cole shakes his head defiantly in my peripherals.

"She put in her Will that I would be legal guardian of him years ago."

Ferguson sighs, as if explaining this is a waste of his time. "Even if that were the case, the courts must still determine you're fit to be his legal guardian." His eyes fixate on Cole. "We will need to speak with you both separately, and based on that initial interview, we will make a determination then."

My hands tremor as I squeeze them into fists, and I glance from Ferguson to the two officers at his sides.

*How can I argue against the legal system?*

*Unless I'm suddenly bulletproof, I don't have a choice here.*

"Okay." I see Cole's head snap to me from the corner of my eye. "Where do we do this interview?"

One officer steps forward with his hand outstretched toward us as Ferguson answers. "We'll go to the station, conduct the interviews, and then determine our next steps from there."

The look on my face must scream nervousness or terror because his detached demeanor fractures. "If everything checks out, we'll send you home with your brother, Ms. Leclair."

Holding his gaze, I nod before following them down the hallway.

*God only hopes it's that easy.*

I watch from the car as officers usher Cole into the police vehicle, which then backs out of its parking spot, and my heart feels like it's in my throat as I hit the call button on the dial pad.

The oppressively loud ringtone fills the space of the car as I follow the cruiser onto the main road.

"Az?"

The sound of Vassago's voice sends a nervous shiver down my spine, which is a welcomed change to the numbness of the past hour.

"Vassago, I–" My words get caught as I pause, still half unsure why I called him at this time of night. With that thought, I look at the clock on the dash, and snap somewhat back to reality.

"I'm so sorry to call you, I just–"

*I just what? What the hell could I say to him that will make any sense?*

*Mom died?*

*Cole's being taken from me?*

*Nothing will make it any better or change the outcome.*

*He's an attorney, not a magician.*

"Az, talk to me. What's going on?"

His voice is like velvet to my ears, and I exhale a ragged breath.

"She's gone, Vassago."

The moment his name leaves my lips, the fracture in the wall around my emotions webs out further.

"I'm so incredibly sorry. Is there anything I can do? Do you need anything?"

The thing about being the sibling that acts as the parent is that you avoid asking for help at every turn. For so long, I just handled everything, never considering the hardship or what I gave up.

For Cole, it was all worth it.

And for him, I can do this.

"Vassago, CPS is interviewing Cole and I at the police station to determine if he can remain with me until the courts process mom's Will." Each word comes out more rough than the last until the emotion I've been holding back finally breaks through, and tears stream down my cheeks. "I don't–"

My voice cuts off with a strangled sob as I come to a red light behind the cruiser.

"It'll be okay, Az. Everything will be okay. Just take a deep breath–" A car horn blares as someone doesn't make a right turn right away. "Are you driving right now?"

I nod, even though he can't see me. "I'm following the police to the station."

There's a long moment of silence before he speaks. "Okay, I'm going to make a few calls. Go do the interview, and cooperate with them. No matter what happens, just trust me, okay? I promise, it will be okay."

Tears continue to stream down my cheeks, and I swipe at them. "Okay. Thank you, Vassago."

"You, of all people, never have to thank me, Az."

# Chapter 18

The interview was shorter than I expected.

I've sat far longer in this uncomfortable chair waiting for an update than it would have taken to do the interview fifty times over.

Checking the time on the wall near the door, I chew the inside of my cheek when I realize it's been nearly two hours since we arrived, and no one's talked to me since the interview ended.

*They wouldn't deem me unfit, would they?*

The questions were straightforward, and I have an adequate job to pay the bills. Cole was happy living with me and mom, and he didn't want to leave me at the hospital.

*What if he changed his mind?*

I shove those thoughts away before blowing out a breath, but footsteps down the hallway grow near, and the door creaks open.

Ferguson steps inside the room, his expression guarded as a wave of nausea washes over me. "Ms. Leclair, there's no easy way to break this to you–" He pauses for only a mere moment, and I'm frozen in place. "Based on our interview and preliminary findings, we've determined that your brother should technically be under your father's custody legally. After hearing a handful of his experiences with your father, we've concluded that a more thorough investigation is required."

*What does he mean? Jeffrey is supposed to be dead.*

*Does this mean that he's alive out there still?*

His jaw ticks, and I track the movement. "With the type of trauma you've both experienced, it's safe to say we have concerns. Since we need to investigate more, Cole will continue to be in the state's custody until we can determine who he would be best off with."

*No. No, this can't be right.*

My chest gets tight, and my breathing picks up, but it's all I can do to focus on keeping my lungfuls even.

Ferguson knocks on the door twice before a tall, dark-haired man with vibrant blue eyes steps inside, accompanied by a shorter woman with long, dark brown hair. Not that I usually judge people at first glance, but these two have an air of calm around them that I desperately cling to.

"Ms. Leclair, this is one of our foster couples who–at quite a short notice–have agreed to take Cole into their care for the intermittent future. It's not typical that you'd get to meet them, but considering the circumstances, they actually requested to."

I frown at him, but I don't have time to comment before the woman steps forward.

"Hello. My name is Oriana. It's nice to meet you."

My eyes gravitate to her extended hand, and I apprehensively shake it before clearing my throat. "Nice to meet you."

My voice is hardly more than a whisper, and my anxiety is nearly at its peak as Oriana glances at her partner, who steps closer to shake my hand as well.

"Name's Seir. It's nice to meet you, Azura."

"Nice to meet you as well." Tears brim in the corners of my eyes as I consider that my little brother will be temporarily part of an actual family.

*Maybe it's best that he's with them and not me.*

*Silver linings and all. That's something he deserves.*

"I'm sorry, I–" My hand quickly shoots to my mouth as the tears spill over, and Ferguson awkwardly looks away.

"It's quite alright, Ms. Leclair." Oriana moves to put her hands on my shoulders in an act of comfort and I suddenly tense, with my breath suspending in my lungs.

Her hands drop to her sides, and her face falls. "I lost my parents in a car accident when I was young. Trust me when I tell you, you have no reason to apologize to us for anything."

Oriana's expression is genuine and screams nothing but pure understanding as Ferguson turns his attention to me.

"To make this as painless as possible, they suggested for you to come see their house, and help your brother feel more comfortable during the transition. It's rather unconventional, but, would you be amenable to that?"

I swallow hard, glancing between the three of them before nodding my head. "Um, sure, I guess."

*What choice do I have?*

I'm not about to let people suddenly whisk Cole away without knowing where he's going or seeing the home he's staying in.

If I have to camp outside their house to make sure he's okay, I will.

Ferguson claps his hands together as if relieved. "Wonderful. Molly was processing the paperwork not long ago, so once we get your signatures, you'll be on your way."

"So–" He freezes mid-turn to look at me. "I'm free to go, then?"

The wry chuckle he lets out makes me want to shrink into nothing. "You were always free to go, Ms. Leclair. You simply weren't free to take your brother with you."

In my peripherals, Seir's jaw ticks just as Oriana's brow twitches, and something twists in my gut at how bluntly he said it in front of them.

"Right," Oriana breathes, gesturing to the door. "Well, we aren't getting any younger. Let's find your brother and we'll get him situated."

Following the trio out the door, we continue down a hallway into the main office, stopping at a desk where a woman types furiously across her keyboard.

"Molly, the paperwork, please."

She hands over a stack of papers that Ferguson thumbs through before handing two papers to me, and a stack to Seir and Oriana. It's not until I skim over the two of mine that I realize both are release of custody forms, and a knot forms in my stomach.

*Is this normal?*

Oriana steps in close, glancing at the papers in my hands before turning to Molly. "Where is the petition for temporary custody for her?"

I blink as Molly stammers. "Oh uh, ah, yes, it's right here."

She passes over another handful of papers that Oriana hands to me with a slight grin.

"I–Thank you."

Her expression softens, and she glances between Seir and me. "We're basically extended family right now, no thanks needed."

My mouth snaps shut, and I'm at a loss for words as I nod.

This couple owes me nothing. Why would they be so nice?

By the time we're done, I've thoroughly reviewed the paperwork before signing, and it's another thirty minutes gone. I'm desperate to see Cole as we head down the hallway lined with offices, and with each step, I'm more and more eager to see him.

We round the last corner to the waiting area, and Cole springs to his feet, running over to hug me tight enough that I have difficulty breathing.

"They won't let me come home?" He murmurs into my hair before releasing me and taking a step back. My chest tightens, and I shake my head as a guarded expression crosses his features.

I know with everything in my heart that he's going to the worst place inside his own mind, but there's nothing I can do to ease it.

Not when I can't bring him home with me.

Ferguson sets the signed paperwork into a folder and tucks it into his side. "Cole, this is Seir and Oriana. You'll be temporarily staying with them until the courts work through your mom's Will or the petition is granted."

"How long could it take for that to happen?"

I feel three sets of eyes burning into the side of my head as Ferguson shrugs.

"Depends on the courts. It could be weeks, could be months, or worst-case scenario, years."

*Years. Shit.*

"Well, let's go then. Most of us aren't going to live forever."

Oriana's hand shoots to cover her mouth at Seir's statement, muffling quiet laughter before humming in agreement.

Something about them is so lighthearted and genuine, it's hard not to like them. I don't know how I feel about that.

"Are you okay to follow us to the house?"

My gaze finds Oriana's and I nod. "Yeah, sure."

Cole's hand slides into mine as we walk out the front doors to the parking lot where a black mustang with dark tinted windows is. The break in the cloud cover casts rays of light against the glimmering dark paint before clouds darken the area once more.

"It's about a thirty-minute drive," Oriana tilts her head slightly and her lips twitch up. "But we should get there in no time." She pulls open the passenger door of the mustang before climbing in, and it rumbles to life loudly.

Thirty minutes. In some cases, thirty minutes could be an eternity, but in all the times when it matters, thirty minutes is never enough.

By the time we're in the car and following Seir's mustang, my chest is tight, and the sweat in my palms makes my grip on the wheel slick.

My eyes find the clock on the dash, and the ball of emotion clogging my throat only grows as the time ticks by another minute.

*Twenty-nine minutes left.*

# Chapter 19

"We don't have to go."

My hand tightens on the wheel as I watch Oriana and Seir climb out of the mustang, chattering quietly no more than fifteen feet in front of the car.

"Of course we have to, Cole."

I hear him take a deep breath. "What if I don't want to?"

My heart rattles against my chest, and my lungs fill faster as I glance from the mustang to the empty driveway.

For a moment, I consider what it would be like to just run away with him.

We'd drive until we were out of gas, with the police surely on our tail, maybe even a warrant for my arrest for kidnapping.

If we were lucky, we'd find somewhere to lie low, but with what money? What resources do we have to sustain ourselves?

The more probable situation is that the police would catch us long before we made it far, and Cole would wind up with Oriana and Seir, anyway.

That's not even considering how much I don't want to go against what Vassago said earlier.

My gaze flicks to where the couple stand murmuring to one another and my chest tightens.

"I have to believe this is only temporary, Cole. Who knows, maybe they're great and this will be like a–I don't know–vacation from life."

Cole scoffs, surging out of the vehicle, and I jolt when the door slams shut. Tears well in my eyes, and I turn my head toward the large house as the garage door opens.

Movement in my peripherals catches my attention and I follow the way Seir and Oriana turn toward the road before my gaze slides in the same direction.

A grey mustang almost identical to Seir's pulls alongside them before coming to a stop. When Vassago comes into view as he climbs out of the driver's side, relief washes over me like a warm blanket.

He smiles warmly at them before his attention turns to Cole, and his features suddenly turn more serious. I'm only half aware of the tears running down my face as I watch him approach Cole and murmur something to him.

Whatever he said has Cole suddenly sobbing, and my eyebrows shoot up as Vassago hugs him while Oriana and Seir walk over to comfort him too.

The four of them look like they could be family with how they're embracing one another, and I've never felt like more of an outsider in my life as tears continue to spill onto my chest.

*Maybe it's best for them if I just go.*

I can arrange mom's funeral, and Cole can have a normal life for once.

He would hate me. He'd blame me for abandoning him.

But he'd have a family.

A life.

He'd have a future.

Stability.

Another fracture in the wall around my emotions cracks, and my forehead drops to the wheel as I desperately choke down the sob in my throat.

I could never give Cole a family like this, or a home that feels so complete.

Seir and Oriana seem like good people, and if Vassago already likes them...

My breath catches in my lungs as a gentle knock sounds out at my window, and I glance over to see the grey of Vassago's suit before swiping the tears from my face.

The door opens, and it feels like my heart could beat from my chest.

"Az."

Each breath feels like a battle as I fight to maintain composure against the emotions warring in my body, but the moment my gaze locks with his, I lose control.

The sob breaks free, and my head drops into my palms as the tears pour out of their own volition.

Mom's gone. I'm losing Cole. Blackwell is surely going to fire me for my absences.

How could this happen? What did I do to deserve this?

Vassago murmurs something under his breath before I feel his arm across my torso, and the click of my seatbelt fills the air before the material disappears from my chest.

My lap is soaked from tears, and I use my sleeves to wipe my eyes as Vassago's voice reaches my ears.

"May I?"

With my body still trembling, I hesitantly glance at where he kneels alongside the door, his arms poised as if he stopped himself just before helping me out of the car.

His grey eyes track the movement of a stray tear down my cheek, and I nod, bringing his attention back to me before he leans in.

I'm half expecting him to just pull me into a hug, but his arm hooks under my knees, with the other encircling my back as he lifts me from the vehicle.

Suddenly, being airborne has my eyes widening, and a jolt of adrenaline surges through me as I'm being lifted. The ease with which Vassago pulls me into his chest as he stands settles my nerves, if only for a moment.

His arms tighten around me as he closes the door with his foot, and walks toward the house as I frown slightly.

"Where are we going?" My voice is hardly more than a whisper as he continues toward the front door.

From this distance, I can see each stubble of hair along his jaw, the way his throat bobs as he swallows, and the muscles that flex along his shoulders and neck as he carries me.

"Inside. My brother is going to make dinner while you two get situated. Though, this is a new rental property for them, so I doubt he'll have any clue where anything is."

I blink, and my brows pinch together as a grin forms in his expression. It's not until his gaze finds mine that he laughs in earnest.

"Did you think I was going to just let some random family get guardianship of your brother? On one of the most important days of your lives? I may be many things, but I'm not a monster."

Ori. He called his sister-in-law Ori. Oriana.

*Holy shit.*

"How?" It's the only word I can muster as the door opens, and Oriana looks apprehensive as Vassago carries me past her.

I feel him shrug as he navigates the house with practiced ease, footing another door open before setting me down gently on a cushioned chair beside a bed.

"The 'how' doesn't really matter, does it? Of all the things you want to know, it's the 'how' that's most pressing to you?"

The look he's giving me feels as if he's setting me up for asking the thing that's been plaguing my thoughts since we went for coffee, and my chest feels tight at the thought of asking it.

Because he's absolutely right.

The how doesn't matter. Even if it was illegal, I wouldn't give a shit how he did it, I'm just thankful that he did.

But there is another question that I'm not sure if I have the courage to ask.

I desperately want to know the answer, though, and my desperation may just win the battle for me.

His grey irises search my face as he patiently waits for me to gather my thoughts, and with each passing moment, my breathing picks up.

If I ask this, and he comes to me with a different answer than what my heart wants...

But if I don't ask, I'll never know.

*Fuck.*

"Why?" My voice is hardly more than a whisper, but it sounds so much louder in my own ears than I expect it to.

One word encompasses it all.

Why are you helping us so much?

Why do you care?

Why did you want to go for coffee when it wasn't necessary?

Why are you always a phone call away?

Why do you invest so much time into my problems?

Why do I feel the way I do about you?

Why do I want you to feel the same way, too?

He adjusts his position to grip the seat on either side of me and brings his gaze level with mine. "When my brother met Oriana, he told me that there was something about her that was just different, and that he couldn't bring himself to be away from her. For weeks I thought he'd gone mad."

He laughs slightly and his eyes drop to the floor before he blows out a breath. When he tilts his head to look at me again, my stomach flips and butterflies soar chaotically through my body. "But then you walked into my office, and it felt like I was standing on the edge of a cliff, looking out into the most beautiful soul that would change my life irrevocably."

The way he speaks has my pulse hike suddenly, and I'm still in disbelief of what he's saying as he continues.

"When you left my office, I dove head-first into research. I was awake for thirty-four hours simply because I needed to make sure I was getting a head start. But then you called me, and the first thing I heard was crying. I've never felt more helpless than I was then, sitting in my car, and unable to fix what was unfolding. For the first time in my life, I finally understood what Seir rambled on about for weeks. Every moment I could be there for you felt like a desperate gamble because I realized that I would give the world to see you smile the way you did when we went for coffee. I've felt myself near obsessed with gathering everything I could about this case simply because of you."

He reaches over to tuck a lock of hair behind my ear, and when I lean into his touch without thinking, emotion flickers across his face. "So to answer your question, Azura Leclair, you would need to look inward, because the answer is you."

My heart feels like it's soaring above the clouds, somewhere in the stratosphere, but at the mention of my case, my mind sobers.

"If we... what would happen to the case if—" My voice cuts off, because I don't know how to verbalize my question.

His jaw tenses. "I don't know."

The air catches in my lungs, and he takes my hands into his as my heart swells almost painfully.

"I won't risk losing the case, because I'm aware of how important it is, but Az—" His voice cracks, and something inside of me feels like it's breaking and melding together all at once. "I've tried, but I can't stay away. Maybe this makes me crazy–Hell knows I feel crazy–but for the life of me, I can't do it. I would welcome death's cold embrace if it only meant seeing you live."

He searches my face, and I know in the depths of my heart that I feel the same. Every moment of weakness, he's been there to catch me, and he's the only person I've ever wanted to turn to.

I lean forward to press my forehead to his, inhaling the scent of his cologne as his free hand slides around the nape of my neck. Our breaths mingle, and our noses brush against each other.

My hand squeezes his and I hold his gaze, with my voice only a whisper. "So don't stay away."

Emotion flickers across his face, and I close the distance between us, pressing my lips to his as my stomach tumbles. His fingers flex in my hair and I realize kissing him was a mistake.

We pull apart for a breath of a moment before his lips press against mine with more urgency, mirroring the growing desire I feel in my core.

A long moment passes that's nowhere near long enough, and he pauses, pulling back ever so slightly to place kisses along my cheek and jaw. At some point I'd leaned in even further, and my cheeks burn at the thought that my entire body itself craves him that much.

"It's official," I whisper. "I never want to leave this room."

His grey irises search mine for a moment, and he places another kiss to my lips. I can tell he's not taking my words as literal, so I double down.

"I mean it, Vassago. I've never wanted someone like–" My voice wavers, and I'm silently thankful, because how could I tell him that I've never wanted someone in such a visceral way. "I don't know what this will mean for us, for the case, but all I know is that I'm worse off without you."

# Chapter 20

Vassago's eyes are wide. "Az, I can't promise it won't be hard at times, I'm—"

Shaking my head, I know I won't need the escape route out of this that he's offering to me. "I'm sure, Vassago."

His mouth snaps shut, and a clatter sounds out from the other side of the house as he chuckles. "Leave it to my brother to break the entire kitchen the one time he needs to cook something."

I can't help but laugh with him, and he gets a thoughtful look on his face before pushing to his feet. "Why don't you go see your brother, make sure he's okay and settled while I make sure Seir doesn't burn anything."

Guilt rifles through me when I realize I left Cole to his own devices here for my selfishness, and Vassago must see it written on my face as he helps me to my feet.

"Your brother was okay when I talked to him earlier. I told him Seir and Oriana are my family. He was relieved and cried, but he was okay."

I nod and blow out a breath. "Thank goodness. He's been through so much–"

Vassago turns, keeping one hand wrapped around mine as he leads us to the door. "You both have, and it's about time for you to breathe easier." He holds the door open and pauses. "The living room is down the hallway to the left. I have to run to my room before going to the kitchen, but let me know if you need me, alright?"

Without a second thought, I release his hand only to step closer, wrapping my arms around his torso as he encircles my shoulders tightly.

"Thank you, Vassago."

I feel his cheek rest against my hair as he squeezes me into him ever so slightly. "You, of all people, never need to, Az."

I'm still reeling from my conversation with Vassago when I turn the corner to the living room, where Cole is flicking through the guide.

"I've never seen over fifty channels before."

He jolts at the sound of my voice and twists to look at me with wide eyes before dropping the remote as it clatters to the ground. He scrambles off the couch before pulling me into a hug.

He sniffs twice before pulling back with a scrunched face. "You smell like Vassago's cologne."

I laugh–really laugh–and roll my eyes. "Yeah, well, so do you, kiddo."

He recoils with a pinched nose before turning his head both ways to sniff his shoulders. "Ugh, I don't smell it."

The laugh that escapes me is unexpected but quiet, and I shake my head, walking over to the couch before flopping down onto it. A few seconds later, he joins me as commercials play on the TV.

"So, are you dating now?"

My cheeks burn, and my mouth drops open to answer, but the look he's giving me says he already knows what I'm about to say, so I just nod.

*"Welcome back to Channel Five News. I'm Casey Warner, here with Ambassador Lor, one of five spokespersons of the magic wielders here on earth..."*

My head turns to the TV where a man with sun-kissed skin and buzzed hair smiles warmly at the camera.

"Did he just say magic wielders?"

I glance at Cole, who's staring at the screen with pinched brows.

*"Ambassador Lor, I know you've come onto various platforms in the last thirty years since magic wielders returned, but what can you tell our viewers about the recent strife?"*

Ambassador Lor nods, looking oddly comfortable being questioned about something so ridiculous.

*"Well, Casey, for a while the general public was getting used to life without the help of magic wielders and for so long, there was tension for various reasons. That tension has come to a head in the United States as more magic wielders have gone missing, and many are blaming the government or a branch of it, while others aren't sure what to think. Either way, it needs to be a topic of a larger conversation, that magic on earth is here to stay, and we need to find a way to live with one another without driving division between our species."*

I click the information button on the remote, seeing a pop-up for Channel Five News stating that there are twenty minutes left.

"This has to be a comedy skit or a movie, right? There's no magic on earth."

"No magic that you're aware of," Oriana's voice fills the air behind us before she steps up alongside the couch. "Most people who are aware of its existence live in the larger cities or where the portals to their realm are, so they see more of them. Tiny towns like ours have divisional leadership with control over most of the media, so these channels aren't usually available."

My eyebrows shoot up. "You're pranking us."

When she just laughs quietly under her breath, I turn my gaze to the television once more to see someone hovering their hand over a strawberry plant as it blooms within seconds before small berries erupt from the flowers, quickly growing into larger, juicy fruits.

"Incredible." I breathe, and Oriana hums in agreement.

"How are you two holding up?" She asks quietly as Cole and I glance at one another.

"Given the circumstances, we're okay, largely because of you and Seir, so thank you for that."

She grins and shrugs. "We owed Vassago a favor, but I'm glad we were able to help. The rest was all him. We just showed up." My eyebrows shoot up again, and she laughs at my reaction. "I'm glad you're both doing alright, then, but I wanted you both to know I'm incredibly sorry for your loss."

The empathy in her eyes is genuine, and I don't need to ask to know she's reminded of losing her own parents as she sucks in a deep breath. "Food should be ready soon if either of you plan to wash up, now's the time. Meet you in there."

She leaves the room, and silence hangs heavily in the air before Cole and I lock eyes.

"Guess we have a lot to learn, huh, kiddo?"

He rolls his eyes with a huff. "How old will I be before you stop calling me that? I'm fourteen. I'm turning fifteen soon."

"You'll be one hundred, and in a home by the time I stop."

He laughs before we both fall silent, with just the news playing in the background. I'm fully aware we're both avoiding the elephant in the room. The elephant being mom's death, but I can't seem to bring myself to knock him down from the tentative comfort he has right now.

"Hey Az."

My gaze flicks at him, and a heaviness weighs on me at the serious look on his face.

"What is it?"

He chews the inside of his lip nervously. "That field trip is in two days. Should I still go?"

I frown. "Do you want to?"

My question must take him off guard as he blinks. "Uh, yeah. I mean, I'd like to, but I don't want to leave you alone, especially not now."

I shake my head and push to my feet. "I'll be fine. If you want to go, I fully support it. Though, I think you'll need Seir and Oriana to sign off on it now."

He rolls his eyes and follows me into the hallway as I pause, looking in each direction.

"Wait, where is the washroom?"

The laugh that escapes him is genuine as he grasps my hand and tugs me to the left. It's mere seconds before we're in the washroom and I shake my head.

"I never would have found this."

"Maybe I shouldn't go to that field trip after all."

Flicking his ear, he laughs and washes his hands before I do the same. The lighthearted moment feels surreal amidst everything that has happened, and by the time we're in the kitchen, the delicious smell of food wafts over, but there's also an underlying scent of something burning that has my nose scrunching.

Oriana must notice as we reach the table where her, and Vassago are already sitting, because she bursts out laughing.

"I'm so glad I'm not the only one who can smell it." Vassago groans. "My dearest Ori here was trying to say this is how it **should** smell when someone cooks."

She just shrugs. "You need to trust the process."

His eyebrows shoot up. "I'll trust that my brother doesn't know what the dials on a stove are for, never mind how that translates to cooking temperatures."

Cole slides into the seat between me and Oriana with a huff of laughter. "Just be thankful he hasn't burned a box of macaroni and cheese before ever getting to cook the noodles."

I gape at him. "I was tired!"

He laughs even harder just as Oriana's hand shoots to cover her mouth.

"You were tired. We almost died. Poe-tay-toe, Poe-tah-toe."

I roll my eyes, crossing my arms over my chest as I lean back. "You did not almost die. The alarm went off. We all woke up. It was fine."

Vassago and Oriana burst out laughing as Seir walks in the room with a platter in each hand.

From the looks of it, not only did he make steak and eggs for breakfast, but there's a platter of pancakes with an assortment of fruit carried in a bowl in the crook of his arm.

How he's carrying all of this and makes it look easy, I'll never know.

"Brunch, anyone?" The brightness in his blue eyes nearly looks like they're sparkling as he grins at us.

"Yeah," Cole says with his eyebrows raised. "This is much better than burnt macaroni and cheese."

My eyes narrow on him as I suck on my tooth. "I'll remember this next time you're hungry at two in the morning."

"Does that happen often?" Oriana muses as she snags a pancake onto her plate.

"No."

"Yes."

Cole and I glare at one another before the others laugh, and I spoon some fruit onto my plate.

"So what do you do for work, Azura?"

My attention turns to Oriana as she takes a bite of her pancake.

"I work at Blackwell law firm as his receptionist." I pause to consider recent events and wince. "At least, for now, anyway."

Seir tilts his head, and his hair shifts with the movement. "What do you mean 'for now'?"

"He hasn't been great about me taking time off while mom is–was–sick." I feel Cole's eyes on me after the correction, but I avoid looking at him as I continue. "I have a feeling my next working shift may very well be my last there."

"What an asshole." Oriana grumbles as she sets her fork down, and I nod.

"Yeah, he's a piece of work. I felt like I owed it to mom to see it through, though. She had Father Arrenault pull strings to get me in, so if I failed him, it was like I was failing her."

Seir and Vassago listen intently, but my gaze remains on a stiff Oriana who looks like she might very well be able to see through to my soul with the way she's staring at me.

"Were you and your mother close?"

I feel myself wanting to close myself off at Vassago's question. The beginnings of shutting down emotionally bubble to the surface, and I fight the urge to give one-word answers.

"Not exactly." I'm half-aware of Cole frozen beside me as I struggle to find the words. "Things were strained for the longest time, but to no fault of hers. She was the breadwinner, so she wasn't around a lot."

Oriana nods slightly, and judging from the look on her face, I already know what she'll ask next.

"And your father?"

In my peripherals, I see Cole's knuckles turn white around his fork.

"He wasn't much of one."

That's the best answer I can give her without going into detail that would expose Cole more than I need to, and thankfully, she seems to get the hint as she glances between us.

"So he wasn't around much? Or he was a dick?"

Okay, maybe she didn't get the hint.

I open my mouth to respond, but Vassago beats me to it as he leans forward. "Fathers are a pain in the ass if you ask me, isn't that right, Seir?"

The dark-haired man across the table looks at me with an expression I can't quite place before he snaps back into the present and turns to Vassago.

"Pain is a colorful word, but I was going to go with a God-given thorn in my side."

Vassago grins. "Poe-tay-toe, poe-tah-toe."

They fall into idle chatter amongst themselves, but I can feel the anxious energy rolling off of Cole beside me as he sits unmoving at the table.

He's always hated when Jeffrey would come up in conversation, and I can only imagine how much worse he feels with mom gone. My gaze lifts to his face, but before I can say anything to him, he surges to his feet.

"Thank you for lunch. Excuse me."

He storms out of the room, and silence hangs heavily around us as I glance at the others. There's a mix of apprehension and guilt across each of their faces, and I know I owe them some kind of explanation.

"Was it what I said earlier?" Oriana's voice is soft, and she seems so much smaller than her usual bright self as I sigh.

"He doesn't like when Jeffrey is brought up."

A sudden flash of realization crosses her features before guilt takes over her expression once more. "Oh god, I'm so sorry."

Shaking my head, I push to my feet. "There's no way you would have known, but I should go check on him."

I move to grab my empty plate, but Vassago halts my hands in place.

"Don't worry about these. Go see your brother."

Tossing him a grateful look, I hurry to find Cole, still unsure which room is his as I navigate through the house until I spot a closed door down the hallway.

By the time I get to it, I can hear sniffles from inside, and I knock three times in a rhythm only we would recognize before easing the door open.

He's laying on his back staring at the ceiling as tears stream from his eyes. "Will I ever not feel fear when I think of him?"

My chest tightens because I know exactly what he means as I pace to the bed and crawl in alongside him.

"If it's not fear, it's anger, or guilt." I whisper, running my fingers through his hair. "I felt fear for the longest time, and sometimes I still do. But most of the time I just feel anger."

His eyes flutter shut, and he shakes his head. "I wish I felt anger."

"No, you don't."

The lump in my throat grows as he turns onto his side. "Tell me how feeling scared every night that he's going to show up is better than anger, Az."

I blow out a breath, turning onto my side and propping myself onto an elbow.

"Fear keeps you alert and watchful. My anger does nothing but make me abrasive and headstrong. It forces me to make decisions on a whim. It makes me reactionary, and because I never have an outlet, all I do is cry."

As if to emphasize my point, the tears brimming in my eyes spill over onto the bed.

"I cry when plans go sideways, I cry when I can't control the situation, I cry when people take advantage of their power and I'm helpless to it, and most of all, I cry whenever any of it has to do with you." The tears continue to fall, and my nose runs, but I push on. "And it's all because I just feel so much anger toward everything that happened to you, while I just stood there, unable to stop it."

Drops of tears fall from his eyes as he shakes his head. "You couldn't have, Az. You were so young–"

"So were you, kiddo."

He searches my face for a moment before leaning in and wrapping his arms around me, and we both shudder.

"I promise I'll always protect you, Az."

My heart feels like it's shattering to pieces as I nod against his hair.

"I promise I'll always do the same, Cole."

# Chapter 21

A sudden loud snore jolts me awake, and my heart beats hard in my chest as I glance around the dark room.

I'm not sure when we fell asleep holding one another, or how long it's been that we've been asleep, but my body feels stiff now that I'm awake, and I'm far too warm for comfort, so I ease off the bed.

My still half-asleep legs wobble as I quietly shuffle to the door and slip out, turning the handle before gently shutting it and letting the knob turn until it clicks in place.

The events of the day and the exhaustion crashes over me all at once as I lean my head against the door frame.

*Just one day at a time.*

Blowing out a breath, I turn to walk down the hallway and take small measured steps toward the living room. By the time I turn the corner and squint against the bright LEDs of the television, it's clear I wasn't the only person who decided it would be a good idea to fall asleep to background noise.

In the shorter loveseat, Vassago's tall form leans awkwardly over the shoulder as he takes even breaths. He looks so incredibly peaceful, even if he looks like he'll wake up with a crook in his neck.

Glancing at the longer couch, I chew the inside of my lip thoughtfully.

What are the chances he's like Cole, and I can wake him up just long enough to convince him to move to somewhere more comfortable?

I assess the two couches for another long moment before approaching the front of the couch. By the time I'm leaning over him, my hand prods him ever so slightly, and his eyebrows pinch together.

"Vassago." My voice is a low whisper, and I prod him once more when he hardly budges. "Vassago, come lay over here."

His eyes scrunch before they open a sliver, and he moves as if on autopilot in the direction I'm guiding him. It's not until he plops onto the couch and his arm snakes around my waist that my eyes widen with a fraction of foresight into what's going to happen.

Before I can even process it, he tugs me into him, and I inhale sharply as I'm headed face-first into the back of the couch. At the last second he rolls onto his side, bringing me along with him awkwardly until I'm stuck between him and the back of the couch, with my legs still half over his thighs.

My heart feels like it could burst from my body as his grip around me tightens, though it's not unwelcomed.

Some small part of me that's still not used to physical interaction from anyone other than Cole balks at the sudden closeness, but the other, larger part of me revels in it.

It's everything I wanted with a delivery that I didn't expect.

The air conditioning kicks on, and a chill breeze has goosebumps breaking out over my arms as I relax into Vassago's grip.

Each beat of his heart that I feel against my shoulder has me settling more and more into him until I'm entirely molded into his body. There's something comfortable about being with him that's alarmingly easy.

He's innately disarming to the chaos in my mind, and I'm still having a hard time understanding it.

How could I be so open and vulnerable to a man I just met? Why does he have this effect on me?

Is this what he meant when he bared so much to me earlier?

My mind sorts through his admissions, and my cheeks burn as I yawn silently.

Could this just be what it feels like to find your person?

With my eyes sliding shut, I lean even further into him as he shifts his other arm around me absently until I'm nearly entirely cocooned, and he sighs contentedly.

Whatever this is, it's tomorrow's problem, if it's a problem at all.

Movement stirs me awake, and I turn toward the source as my eyes peel open.

Vassago's mussed, dirty-blonde hair is the first thing I notice before his half-lidded eyes meet mine.

"Sorry for waking you."

Even his sleep-laden voice is rich, and I shake my head.

"I'm sure I was about to wake up soon, anyway." I yawn, and he glances around before I see the realization dawn on him.

"How did we end up on this couch?" The question in his expression is genuine, as if he was truly half asleep when I tried to move him, and I fail to suppress a laugh.

"I tried to move you somewhere more comfortable. Sleepy Vassago decided there was room for two."

His cheeks turn a tinge of pink. "I crossed a boundary, Az. I don't even remember–"

"It's fine."

His brows pull together in tense concern as he searches my face. "Are you certain?"

Instead of answering immediately, I think–really think–about how I've felt since I woke up.

There's been no negative reaction or any urge to withdraw into myself at how close we still are. I fell asleep within minutes, and I certainly stayed asleep the whole time.

I'm more rested than I've felt in a while and other than the slight ache in my neck from the way I slept, I feel great considering.

Our gaze locks once more and my lips twitch. "I'm sure."

The relief on his face is clear as day, and he shifts to sit up fully on the couch as a door shuts down the hallway.

"What time is it?"

Vassago pulls his phone from his pocket, and before he can answer, I groan. "I need to get ready for work."

Sitting upright and stretching, my joints pop loudly, and Vassago looks at me with a raised brow.

"It's Sunday, Az. Blackwell's office is closed."

I blink at him, and recount the days in my head before my eyebrows shoot up.

"It feels like this week has been a month long."

The laugh that escapes him is genuine, and I find myself smiling in response, but it quickly fades as I remember what the hospital said the next steps were.

My face falls, and he must notice as he suddenly looks at me with concern etched into his features. "What is it?"

Leaning back into the couch fully, staring at the high ceiling, I release a deep sigh. "I need to start funeral arrangements."

There's a long moment of silence between us as I mentally file through what bits and pieces I can remember from the hospital. Though the numbness may have dulled the pain of losing Mom, it did nothing to help my memory of what I needed to do afterwards.

"Would you like help?"

I quickly turn to look at him, only to find a tenderness in his grey eyes that makes my chest tighten.

I don't deserve this kindness.

"I–"

"I won't take it personally if you decline."

My mouth snaps shut, and I search his face for a moment before nodding. "I have no idea what I'm doing, where to start and what is needed."

Rubbing my hands together, my attention drags to Vassago as he slides his palm into mine, and gives it a slight squeeze.

"Then allow me to help."

# Chapter 22

Six hours.

It took only six hours for Vassago to arrange everything for mom's funeral.

Once he worked with the funeral home director to get the burial permit, selected a handful of caskets but refused to let me see the prices, arranged for a small burial service, he gathered all her important documents, and had insurance companies notified as well as the bank, closed all her credit cards and any other loose ends I'd probably never have thought of.

I've never seen anything like this in my life.

I've also never been so grateful in my existence.

The moment he came to me about caskets, I cried. He suggested flowers for the small service. I cried again.

The funeral home is the only one in town, and Vassago arranged for the service to be Monday morning since Cole leaves for his field trip in the afternoon.

"Okay, here are a few options."

Oriana walks into the room with a handful of hangars, and on each of them is a dark blue or black dress of varying styles with matching cardigans.

"I had to dig deep into my goth girl era for these, so just know they're maybe a little older, but they're still in good shape, considering."

I take the handful of articles of clothing and thumb through them, pausing at one dark dress that has a cinched waist with mid-length sleeves.

Oriana must notice that I paused because she snags the other ones from my hands with a quiet laugh.

"I had a feeling that one would catch your eye." She tosses them on the bed before plopping down beside me. "That one belonged to my best friend a long time ago."

The sadness in her tone has my brows pull together, and I don't miss the way she blinks faster before taking a deeper breath than usual.

"What happened to her?"

She chews the inside of her lip for a moment. "There are demons in this world, Azura. She got too close to them and paid the price."

I swallow hard, and the memory of Jeffrey comes into the forefront of my mind as I shudder. "I'm sorry."

She glances at me before shaking her head slightly. "It was quite some time ago, and as much as I miss her, I'm glad we got justice."

I don't have the heart to ask if that's how she met Vassago, and I'm already assuming he represented her or helped catch them as she clasps her hands to her thighs and pushes to her feet.

"Well, I'm going to go get dinner ready." She pauses, glancing between me and the door. "Do you want to give me a hand?"

My eyebrows shoot up. "After what Cole said earlier, you trust me with a stove?"

She just laughs, offering her hand between us. "Better you than Seir! Come on."

My hand slips into hers, and she tugs me to my feet before leading the way to the kitchen. We get halfway there when I realize that she's still holding my hand as she leads me, and I'm not remotely bothered or shying away from it.

I'm staring at where our hands connect as we turn the last corner to the kitchen, and I hardly register Cole and Seir's voice coming from another room.

Oriana glances toward their chatter before grinning at me and releasing my hand to grab various items from the fridge.

"Seir has always had a way of connecting with people."

I hesitate for a second, and I glance to the hallway before helping bring various veggies to the counter.

"If he can get through to Cole in two days, he will deserve an award."

The grin on her face widens, and she grabs a cutting board. "I'll start looking for trophies for him tonight, then."

I can't help but laugh as we fall into a rhythm of preparing dinner. Cole might be easy to get along with, but he doesn't open up easily, and as much as I'd love for him to feel comfortable with Seir and Vassago, men are not exactly good in his books.

And I'd never fault him for feeling that way, because he's not wrong.

*Maybe someday it will be different.*

*Maybe.*

# Chapter 23

"Dinner is ready!" Oriana leans into the doorway as her voice nearly echoes within the walls themselves.

The sound of footsteps grows closer, and Seir enters the room before Cole and Vassago. The three of them grin ear to ear as they take a seat at the large table and scoops sautéed vegetables onto their plates.

Oriana and I exchange a look with a hint of a smile before following suit.

"Az." Cole jabs a Brussels sprout with his fork. "I need to get clothes for my field trip this week."

Glancing at the clock and groaning internally, I nod. "I'll go get your stuff from the house after dinner."

Silence falls over the table before Seir clears his throat. "Have you decided what you're going to do once you're sick of Blackwell?"

The question catches me off guard, and I chew the inside of my lip. "I actually haven't considered it, but I guess I should. He's not exactly a fan of mine."

Vassago laughs under his breath. "He'd be a terrible fan to have, to be honest. The man has always struck me as someone who stares at the mirror for thirty seconds too long."

My hand shoots to my mouth to muffle my laughter, and Vassago just grins wider at my reaction.

"Is he really that bad?"

I glance at Oriana and grimace. "Yeah, he's pretty obnoxious. He wasn't so bad at first, but for the past year, he's been unlivable."

She looks at Seir for a moment before cutting a piece of chicken. "I wonder what changed."

"Not a clue, but I couldn't care less what the reason is. It's free to be nice."

Seir and Vassago hum in agreement as they continue eating, and I chew slowly as I run through what moving on from Blackwell would look like.

Reception has been my only line of work so far, but I'm certain I could learn any other roles fairly easily. The real question is whether I'll need to get a second job anyway to sustain income for Cole during school or not.

We have enough saved now to get us through on bills for a little while, but the funeral will eat at that nest egg.

That's not even considering the fact that I have no clue how much the arrangements were since Vassago handled everything.

I glance over at him only to find his attention on me, and when our eyes meet, my cheeks burn.

"So, you have a weeklong field trip coming up?"

Cole nods, and I notice the slight flush to his cheeks with a note of suspicion. "Yeah, it's a camping site. Not all kids get to go. It seems fun."

My brows shoot up. "What do you mean not all kids get to go?"

Seir and Oriana exchange a look, and Cole just shrugs. "I dunno. They review which students would benefit the most from the trip and they send out the consent forms."

"Wouldn't more participation be better and inviting more people would achieve that?"

The flush in his cheeks grows, and he shakes his head with a defensive look. "I don't know. Maybe I'm doing well and can afford to miss a week?"

Realizing I'm bothering him, I just nod. "Uh, yeah, that makes sense."

"Well," Seir murmurs. "It can't be any worse than the time Ori tried to convince me to go camping with Vince, and the two of them nearly burned the entire campsite down."

My eyes widen as Ori gasps, gaping at him with a hint of humor in her expression. "How was I supposed to know that Vince threw the lighter into the fire?"

Vassago covers his mouth as he chuckles, and Seir grins ear to ear. "We were in the middle of a mandatory burn ban?"

Oriana flushes bright pink. "They announced it while we were camping!"

Throwing his hands up in surrender, he shrugs with poorly restrained humor painted across his features. "I'm just saying their camping can't go any worse than that."

She sucks her tooth as Vassago finally composes himself, turning to me with a conspiratorial smirk. "My brother seems to forget the time where he set an entire house on fire with fireworks because he refused to read instructions."

Oriana sputters, her wide eyes bouncing between Vassago and Seir. "You hypocrite!"

Seir and Cole both bark out a laugh, and I shake my head with a huff of my own.

The rest of the meal falls into relative normalcy, and I'm grabbing my keys by the back door as Cole helps Seir and Oriana clean the kitchen when Vassago's voice halts me in place.

"Would you like company?" I turn, tilting my head to meet his gaze, and he gently shifts a piece of hair from my eyes.

My heart feels like it could beat from my chest, but my mind goes absolutely blank as I nod. "Sure."

He holds the door open, and I'm immediately aware of every move I make as I brush past him toward the car. The air feels thick with tension, and I'm not sure if I'm just imagining it as part of my delusion.

Everything in me craves more than just his touch, and when my thoughts take a more scandalous turn, I mentally chide myself. The dim light of dusk casts shadows over the driveway and along the treeline as I click the button on the key fob.

It beeps twice as the doors unlock, and I just catch the slight up tilt to his lips as he climbs into the passenger seat.

"Are you always this eager to go for a drive?"

His teeth flash with a grin as he adjusts in his seat, and it takes a conscious effort to remain focused on his face instead of his thighs. "Not always."

My cheeks warm as I put the car into gear and pull out onto the driveway toward the main street.

"You didn't have to come with, you know?"

Silence fills the space, and I glance over at Vassago to find him already assessing me from the passenger seat.

"I never **have** to do anything, Az. I do things because I want to or because they bring me joy. If I didn't wish to, I simply wouldn't."

My brows pull together.

What a life that would be to simply do what I wanted, when I wanted.

My thoughts wander to all the times in my life when I had to make sacrifices, and I find myself reflecting on each of them with a note of bitterness.

Every part of me knows that things could have been worse for us, but it's hard to not wonder what life would have been like had mom just fallen in love with someone other than Jeffrey.

Who knows if Cole would be alive in that reality.

Or myself, for that matter.

Still, there's a chance that there was a future in store for us that didn't involve years of abuse and trauma mixed with personal sacrifices.

"What is it?"

I shake my head. "Nothing."

There's a long moment of silence before Vassago's voice fills the air.

"I suppose that was insensitive of me to say, even if it was the truth."

"You're fine."

My response comes out quick, and it's clear even to me that I'm being dismissive, even though I know he's right.

"If the world was different, and you could do anything you want, what would you choose to do?"

For a split second, I nearly indulge as my mind wanders, but I quickly snap back to reality as I turn off one highway ramp to another, and I shake my head.

"It really doesn't matter what I want, because that world doesn't exist."

"Doesn't it?"

"It doesn't, and if I stop to even think about it for a moment, I will yearn for something I can never have, so I'd really rather not disappoint myself." Silence falls over us, and I release a long sigh. "I'm sorry."

"Never apologize for honesty, Az."

"It may have been honest, but it was also rude."

"Blunt maybe, but not rude." I feel his hand encircle mine, and my lungs nearly seize as I struggle to stay focused on driving. "A long time ago, when my family had their falling out, I think I told you I was a mess."

I nod, feeling his thumb glide along the back of my hand absentmindedly.

"For years, I didn't know what to do with myself. I was in a new place, with little knowledge of the culture, the community, the rules and laws that now applied to me. It felt like I was constantly playing a game of catch up because every other minute I was learning something new that could change the course of my life. I was in New York for a few years, and, if you've never seen New York, the hustle and bustle of life there is unlike most places you'll witness. I was so accustomed to the busy day-to-day that I'd lost sight of what it felt like to stop and just enjoy the moment."

I'm reminded of all the times I'd be doing busy work at home, working and doing chores just to keep myself away from the dreary reality that what I want in life doesn't really matter.

"That was until I met a woman named Nina Schleronov."

Hearing the way his voice softens, I glance at him only to see his eyes distant as he stares out the window with a serene look on his face.

Curiosity burns in my mind, and I ask, unable to stop myself. "Who was she?"

He turns his gaze to me, but mine return to the road before we can make eye contact. "I was walking through Central Park, and she was on a bench painting. I hardly made it past her when she called out to me, and even though I was behind on time, she was insistent that I help her with something. When I asked her how I could help, she told me to sit down, and so I did as she asked. Though, once I sat down, she introduced herself, and didn't say another word."

I chance another look at him, seeing the hint of humor on his face.

"I remained there by her side for five minutes before I wondered if I should speak up. It was ten minutes before I relaxed and observed the scenery, and twenty minutes later I realized she didn't actually need anything. Thirty minutes after I sat down, she turned to me with a smile before asking if I'll come back sometime soon. I never saw her after that, but the peace I felt in that moment has stuck with me. I returned every other day to spend a few minutes on that bench, watching people pass by, and it gave me a fresh perspective."

My throat tightens at the thought, knowing that I likely haven't given myself time to just enjoy a moment like that freely. "What per-spective did it give you?"

The familiar scenery of Dartmouth street comes into view, and my insides flip nervously as Vassago's thumb glides along my hand.

"It allowed me to see that there were other ways to move forward. Paths in life I hadn't considered simply because I was being close-minded. It made the once bleak future turn into endless possibilities, and I wouldn't be in this car at this very moment, on this very day if she hadn't gotten my attention in that park."

The car comes to a stop in the driveway, and he releases my hand as I shift into park before looking at him. "So you're saying that I should pretend that I can somehow magically do whatever I want in life?"

He just smiles slightly, like he knows the world's biggest secret. "I'm saying that you need to dream before you can achieve. Anything is possible, Az."

I fall silent as I get out of the car, internally warring between wanting to allow my mind to wander and reining it in. I'm unlocking the door with Vassago behind me as I consider the day Cole goes to college, not needing my daily, weekly, or even monthly help with anything.

What would I do with my time?

Blackwell's office comes to mind, and I come full circle to the question of what other businesses in town I could apply to work for.

But what if I could do something more impactful?

What would I even want to do?

The news from the other night and the knowledge of magic users tugs on a thread of interest as I chew the inside of my lip.

"I want to travel."

My heart thumps steadily in my chest as I turn to look at Vassago's soft expression, as if he knows the turmoil it's taken me to think of what I would desire.

"Any destinations?"

I shake my head, leading us both down the hallway. "Finding out that there's magic in the world made me realize that there's been so much I've missed. So much that I don't know or need to learn. So no, no destination, but I want to see as much as I can."

Realizing that I accidentally walked past Cole's room and nearly went to my own out of habit, I turn around, bumping right into Vassago's chest. I gasp, and his hands move to my elbows to steady me as I almost lose my footing.

"Let me take you."

His words come out half demanding, but I don't have time to sort through his words as his hand drags up my arm, and he tilts my chin up.

His cologne invades my senses, and I can't breathe as his light grey eyes search my face. With his proximity, it's all I can do to manage one word out. "Where?"

His dark blonde hair falls forward as he leans in, brushing his lips against mine as he whispers. "Everywhere."

He hardly gets the word out before he closes the distance, and the moment he presses his lips to mine, a wave of heat surges through me.

Our lips dance as he walks me backward until my heel bumps the wall, but he continues his advance, melding his body against mine and cupping my jaw with his palms. My heart soars, like every moment I was averse to touch had led me to this as he teases my lower lip between his teeth.

He pauses with his lips still against mine, and I feel his hand move lower down my neck, with the other already firm against my hip.

"That would take a while."

His lips curve into a smile, and he reaches lower to hook his hand under my thigh, pulling it around his waist as I suck in a breath.

"We have all the time in the world, Az."

# Chapter 24

His lips crash against mine, and before I know it, he's gripping my ass with his hands as he hauls me higher against the wall. My legs instinctively wrap around his waist, and the moment he throbs against me, I grind into him in response, and he lets out a husky groan.

"God help me." He slides his arm around my waist and pulls me from the wall, carrying me to my bedroom.

How the hell he knew it was mine, or whether he simply guessed. I have no idea.

Nor do I care.

He walks to the bed and holds me to him as he crawls to the center of the bed and eases me down.

Heat engulfs my body as his gaze travels down the length of me. "You look so good like this, Az–" He kisses down my collar to my chest, nipping at my skin to emphasize each work. "Flushed, needy, and undone."

He tugs my shirt up over my head and kisses down my breasts to my stomach, and I'm hanging on by a thread as he skillfully removes the rest of my clothing, discarding them to the floor.

When I go to grab the hem of his shirt, he grabs my wrists and chuckles, the dark edge to it sends a shiver down my spine.

"Be a good girl for me and stay just like that." He leans back and unbuttons his shirt, exposing the tattoos on his chest that trail down his arms in sleeves as I swallow.

He tosses it aside my thighs clench at the sight of the deep set V line hugging his hips as he unclips his belt with one hand. His pants fall to the floor moments later, and I already feel breathless.

Someone might as well have sculpted his body from art itself. Tattoos accent the corded muscles that flex as he prowls on top of me once more.

He eyes my wrists with appraisal, which have obediently remained in place. "You know how to get what you need, don't you?"

I nod, keeping my hands firmly in place as he crawls up the length of my body. "Yes, sir."

Heat darkens his gaze, and he hums in approval before settling between my legs, and kissing up my collar. "That's my girl." He leans in to tease my nipple with his teeth and I gasp, my legs tensing against his hips.

He throbs against me, and I shiver. My hips move of their own accord, desperate to feel him as he throbs again.

"Vassago–" My words cut off abruptly as he throbs again, and the head of his dick notches against my entrance. When I shudder at the feeling, his breath hitches.

"You're already trembling, Az, and we haven't even gotten started yet."

"Vassago, I need more." I whisper, and my core throbs against him.

He groans with his forehead against my chest. "Az, I am trying to not take you hard and fast right now, but if you keep testing me, I won't be able to stop myself."

Oh, god that's all that I fucking want.

"Please–" My voice is pleading, aching for relief as my hands twitch with the urge to move.

He pushes in deeper, and I feel my body stretch to accommodate his size. The twinge of pain makes my eyes roll back, and a whimper escapes my throat.

"Vassago–"

He grips my throat, and I'm gazing at him through half-lidded eyes as his jaw feathers.

"Say my name again."

My pulse spikes as he withdraws slightly and when I repeat his name, he slams into me, making me cry out.

"Again."

"Vassago," I whisper, and he searches my face as he withdraws to the tip.

"Say it like it's the only word you know, Az." His breath skates over my skin as he pushes in, and my heart's beating a mile a minute with the pressure against my clit.

His name becomes a prayer on my lips as he pumps into me, and every bolt of pleasure radiating from my core has my arms trembling over my head.

Vassago must know I'm close as he thrusts hard, squeezing my clit as his hand fists my hair, tugging my head back. "That's it, beloved. Come undone for me just like that."

My hips snap to his each time he slams in, and I'm begging him not to stop in a language built of a single word when my orgasm crashes into me.

Vassago's clutching me to him, buried so deep that I feel him throb in my stomach as he comes, and he presses his forehead to mine as our breaths mingle between us.

"No one else will ever get to see you undone like this, Az. Not today, not tomorrow, not next year." My heart thunders, and I nod slightly in agreement.

The possessive edge of his voice sends a thrill down my spine, and he withdraws, pressing his lips to mine in a long, drawn out kiss. Moments pass, and he rolls beside me on the bed, tracing lines along my arms as I fight the urge to fall asleep against his chest.

I'm not sure how long we've been in bed, but judging by the way the sky has darkened through the sheer curtains in the window, it must have been close to an hour, and Vassago's phone buzzes on the side table.

He answers and presses it to his ear as a muffled voice comes through. "Tell him I'll be there in thirty." He says with a sigh, and hangs up the phone.

When our eyes meet, he places another kiss against my lips, then my cheek and my hair. "Duty calls. Will you be alright here for a bit by yourself?"

I nod, fighting the urge to ask him to stay. "Define alright."

His lips twitch, and he searches my face before climbing off the bed to put on his clothes. "I'll be back before you know it."

My gaze drops to his open zipper before flicking to his, and heat flashes in warning across his features.

"You better be."

# Chapter 25

The door to mom's room opens inch by inch, and I glance around at her belongings. They're the same as she left them that day, stuck in the moment in time from when she rushed to the hospital.

A small box of her belongings sits on the chair in front of her messy vanity, where her deodorant still lies knocked over from when she hurried out of the room.

Clothes thrown over the bed, shoes kicked to the side and other personal items strewn about only serves to constrict my throat with emotion.

There's no way I can go through her things yet.

Not now.

Tears well in my eyes, and I turn away from her room, shutting the door quietly as I pad over to Cole's. Silence hangs oppressively around me now that Vassago's not here, and I'm halfway through the door when my phone vibrates in my pocket.

Seeing Unknown on the caller ID, I swipe the screen to answer and hold it to my ear.

"Hello?"

Static comes through the speaker, and I frown.

"Hello?"

Another long moment of silence drags on, and I'm about to pull the phone from my ear to hang up when I hear it.

"You think you're safe?"

The voice holds a familiar note I can't quite place, and I frown. "Who is this?"

More static sounds from the speaker and the audio comes through choppy as the person continues. "Do you... –en know who... fucking with?"

*Are they talking to me or did someone butt dial me?*

"I think you have the wrong number."

I'm about to hang up as the line suddenly comes through, clear as day.

"Your pretty boy attorney is evil, dumb bitch. He's a fucking demon."

My eyebrows shoot up. "Okay, who the hell is this?"

The line disconnects, and I pull the phone from my ear only to stare at the screen, replaying what I heard over and over in my mind.

*Could it have been a prank?*

*Something to rattle me?*

It's not surprising to me that Vassago would have enemies, since it's part of the job. One party wins, the other loses.

The surprising part is that someone is coming after me because of their vendetta against him.

How would they even know that we're working together? Has word travelled that fast since that day at the school?

Sliding my phone into my pocket, I walk over to Cole's dresser and pull clothes out, glancing them over before tossing them onto the unmade bed.

The entire house seems as if it's in stasis, and I'm doing nothing more than disrupting the peace with each step, each movement, each article of clothing. My mind wanders back to the phone call as I mindlessly pick outfits for Cole's trip.

Who did Vassago piss off so much that I'm receiving phone calls calling him evil? What did they mean to do by calling **me**? Intimidate me?

The thought of stirring up even more trouble flips my stomach uncomfortably, and I sigh, pulling open Cole's sock drawer to grab a few pairs. I plop them onto the bed and walk over to the closet to get his duffle bag, freezing when a shadow crosses outside the window.

Adrenaline rushes through my veins as my pulse picks up, and my eyes strain for movement beyond the curtains. A quiet thud near the front of the house echoes into the still air and I jolt.

*Was someone in the backyard?*

*First the phone call, now this... is someone following us?*

My body turns to ice as I consider that someone could have heard us earlier, and all the impact that could have on the case.

I need to see who the hell that was.

Within seconds I'm hurriedly tip-toeing to the hall, keeping low as I peer around the corner to the front entryway. A long moment passes, then two, and it feels like my heart could beat out of my chest until a car engine rumbles to life on the front street, and I hurry to the window by the front door.

Peeking out from a gap in the blinds, I watch a white car with dark tinted windows slowly turn onto the road from where it was parked, and it crawls past the house to the main road.

Whoever is driving brakes more in front of the house, and the driver's side window rolls down as the streetlight reflects off of something shiny and metallic.

*Shit.*

I realize what it is and hurl myself to the side. I'm free-falling away from the window just as thundering booms fill the air and glass shatters. My hands instinctively cover my head as I slam hard to the floor, and roll toward the front room, hardly paying attention to the glass that's tearing into my skin. Adrenaline pumps hard through me, and my blood rages in my ears as I finally hit the side of the couch, angling myself flat to the floor as more shots sound out.

My ears ring, but I'm relieved that my hearing is intact as the car's tires squeal, and the engine roars as the driver takes off down the road. My body feels like ice as I tremble uncontrollably, glancing toward the front entry with wide eyes as the engine fades into the distance.

When my gaze lands on the wall directly behind where I stood moments prior, seeing countless holes, my head spins.

Any of those could have hit me.

My focus drops to the floor, where shattered glass lies scattered across the hardwood, mixed with smears of blood, and as I shift to my side to look over my body, my limbs are shaking so much that I'm unable to support my weight.

*I'm okay.*

*All of this is just material. It can be replaced.*

*I'm okay.*

My breathing is labored, and it feels like every breath has been robbed of oxygen as I suck in each one deeper than the last.

*At least no one else was here to get hit.*

Reminding myself that Cole is safe with Seir and Oriana, I fight a wave of nausea that sends bile into my throat. I gingerly push to my knees, cautious to avoid broken glass, before pulling out my phone.

"Hello, Rennensberg 911. What's your emergency?"

"I–" The numbness starts to fade, giving way to the pain lancing throughout my body, and I wince. "My name is Azura Leclair, and someone just shot at my house."

After giving the operator my address and on the verge of tears, my phone beeps, and I see Vassago's name on the caller ID.

"We have a unit heading over to you, Ms. Leclair. Are you hurt?"

I shake my head and open my mouth to respond, but the ripped material in my shirt and the blood that's smeared or splattered all over the floor gives me pause.

"I didn't think so, but I might be. There's blood. Not a lot, but..."

My hands tremor, and another sudden wave of nausea washes over me as I empty the contents of my stomach onto the floor.

"Okay, Ms. Leclair. Officers are almost there, and paramedics are on route to you."

The faint sound of sirens gets louder, and I put the operator on speaker, shakily typing out a text to Vassago.

**Azura:** Something happened at the house. I'll call you after the police and ambulance get here.

Vassago reads the message, but says nothing back as heavy footsteps echo on the front porch.

"Rennensberg Police, we're coming in."

Some rustling sounds out, like someone jostling broken glass before a click, and I realize the officer unlocked the door from the shattered window as it creaks open.

Two officers step into view, glancing around before their attention falls to me, and I go to move, but they place their palms outstretched between us.

"Easy. We're going to check you out to make sure there are no serious wounds that need attention before the paramedics get here."

My nerves are already beyond frayed, and my anxiety skyrockets as I nod, and the officers step closer. One kneels beside me and gingerly begins lifting the hem of my shirt to visually check for injuries; even though I'm fully aware of what they need to do, everything in me wants to pull away.

When an engine roars down the street, my heart thunders.

Could he be back to finish the job? What if it's the shooter?

The sound cuts out and not long after, hurried footsteps fill the air as someone takes long strides up the patio and my anxiety reaches a peak.

It's not until I see Vassago's tall form turn the corner that I take a full breath, seeing the mix of concern and fury in his features as he surveys the holes in the walls.

When his attention slides to where the officers are kneeling at my side, my throat tightens to the point of pain.

"Az." Vassago takes two steps closer just as one officer stands up, holding his palm between them. "Are you alright? What the hell happened?"

The worry in his expression bleeds into what could only be pure rage as he looks over the wood chips jutting from the wall, and the glass pieces on the floor smeared with blood.

"Who are you exactly?"

Vassago turns from me to the officer, and he schools his features, but the worry remains clear in his eyes. "I'm her attorney."

The other officer drops the hem of my shirt and stands up. "Well, she has some minor cuts and scrapes, but she should be okay. Medics should be here in a few minutes to check her out. You can talk to her then. Joffsen, see the attorney out. This is an active crime scene."

Joffsen steps over to Vassago, his hand wrapping around his bicep but Vassago shrugs him off. "Touch me again, Joffsen. You **will** regret it."

Both cops visibly stiffen, but Vassago's oblivious to them as his eyes linger on me. He must decide that complying is the best course of action since he turns to the front door, cautiously stepping around the large pieces of glass.

Once he's out of my line of sight, the incessant hum of anxiety circles my mind in the long minute before two medics turn the corner from the hallway, carrying packs in each of their hands.

The first medic, a younger man with short black hair and dark stubble lining his jaw, looks at me apprehensively before kneeling at my side with his pack.

The lack of distance between us makes me want to crawl out of my fucking skin. If he touches me, I may very well freak out because even with him inches from me, I want to scream. I feel my pulse spike as he methodically opens his bag while his partner asks questions.

"What's your name?"

"Date of birth?"

"Do you know where you are?"

I'm halfway through answering his last question as the medic closest to me reaches over to grab my arm. Instinct takes over as I jerk away, my pulse spiking as they both pause.

The paramedic closest to me rolls his eyes. "We need to check your injuries, Azura."

Each breath fills my lungs, but they somehow still feel starved of oxygen, and I look wildly between them. Everything in me wants to scream for them to stay away, that I'm fine, and I don't want to be touched, but before I can say anything, before I can explain that I don't want to be touched, the medic reaches out again to grab my arm.

This time his grip is bruising, and a million memories of years of rough hands remind my frantic mind that this paramedic is not here to help. Neither of them are here to help or listen.

He lifts my arm, and I desperately jerk my arm in his grasp. My mind goes blank as a wave of panic takes over. "Let me go!"

The officer that didn't escort Vassago outside steps closer and grabs my shoulders before roughly shoving my body hard into shards of glass on the floor.

I fight against the hands gripping my biceps and forearms. Someone is yanking them behind my back at an angle that feels like my joints will pop, and a heavy weight bears down on my shoulders, squeezing the air from my lungs.

My next breath hardly comes, and between it and the panic, I start to feel lightheaded.

"Please." I whisper, and another shallow breath barely reaches my lungs. "Stop."

Each heartbeat feels like it lasts an eternity, and the pressure in my head feels like it's reaching a breaking point.

# Chapter 26

"Release her."

Vassago's voice is cold, commanding, and resolute as the weight disappears from my back. With an eager, desperate breath, I roll away and onto my back, ignoring the glass digging into my skin, realizing my arms are free.

I cough violently when the rush of air is too much all at once, and when my fit slows, I glance between the four men. They stare at Vassago with a look I can't quite place, but it's not until my eyes find him that I understand.

He looks like he's deciding whether he should sue them or kill them.

The tension in the room is palpable, and fury emanates from where he stands, rolling off him as his jaw feathers. The sight sends a shiver down my spine, even though I'm not the subject of his anger. His gaze flicks to me, scanning my body before meeting mine, as the paramedics and officers remain motionless.

I breathe hard, and he must notice as his bright grey eyes track the movement. "Are you alright, Az?"

Nodding lightly, he steps past the four men in the room and offers his hand. They look half-dazed, half-pissed, and the paramedic who grabbed my arm glares in my direction as I accept Vassago's help up.

For whatever reason, none of the men surrounding us move a muscle as Vassago leads me to the doorway with his hand gingerly against the small of my back.

He turns to Joffsen, who seems to snap out of whatever daze he'd been in, glancing between the others apprehensively.

"My client will make a statement through me. Do whatever investigation you need to find the culprit, but you will no longer have direct access to her without me present." He turns his attention to me, and the hard look in his eyes melts away. "Did you get all of Cole's stuff packed?"

In the chaos of everything, I'd completely forgotten why I came to the house to begin with.

I nod as he leads me out the front door, and more sirens grow closer. "It's all in the duffel bag in his room."

We're nearly at the car when he reaches for the passenger handle and leans in close. "Keep the door locked. Don't open it for anyone."

He doesn't have to tell me twice.

I slide into the passenger seat with a wince, clipping on my seatbelt as the door shuts, and all the locks click into place with two quiet beeps.

The quiet surrounding me is comforting, even with the siren growing closer until a large white SUV pulls up to the house, and the sound cuts off.

The door opens, and an older man with a shaved head climbs out before moving to the side door, sliding it open and rummaging around.

I'm caught up watching him when a knock at my window jolts me, and I gasp, looking with wide eyes at Joffsen and one paramedic crowding the door.

Joffsen leans in to the glass to see through the dark tint, and I instinctively lean away, tossing a cursory glance to the lock that's still in place with relief.

Whatever Joffsen sees—or doesn't—has him clicking his tongue. "Ms. Leclair, we need a word with you."

Vassago's words repeat in my mind over and over as I chew the inside of my cheek nervously.

Ignoring authority was never a strong suit for me, because growing up, ignoring authority meant punishment.

"Ms. Leclair, open the door or else."

My fingers twitch at the hardly veiled threat, and seconds go by before I watch with wide eyes as Joffsen reaches out to grab the handle, tugging at it.

I know they're probably so insistent about getting to me because they want to know what happened, but after the incident earlier, I can't help but feel even more untrusting of them.

"Step away from my vehicle, Officer Joffsen. In fact, both of you remove yourselves from the passenger door. You are not welcome here."

My neck cracks with how quickly I turn to look at Vassago carrying the filled duffle bag. The trunk beeps as it opens, and a loud thud shakes the car before he shuts it.

Surprisingly, both Joffsen and the medic retreat to their own vehicles, and I nearly sigh with relief as the car beeps and Vassago climbs in.

He scans the surrounding area once before turning his attention to me. "I'm going to kill them."

My cheeks burn, and I huff a dry laugh. "The last thing you need is to be taking on Rennensberg High School in court and simultaneously going to jail for murder."

The laugh that escapes him is genuine, and he flashes a grin while reaching over to press the button to turn the engine on with a loud rumble.

"I never turn down a challenge, Azura. Besides, they'd have to catch me **and** convict me. It would never happen."

My lips twitch, and there's a moment of silence before we turn onto the main road. "I don't understand why this happened."

Vassago presses down on the gas, and I feel myself sink further into my seat as he releases a deep breath. "Without having seen who it was, my only assumption is that it has to do with our case against the school."

My eyes widen, and I stare at him in disbelief. *Is he saying what I think he is?*

"You really think they'd send someone to hurt me? They're supposed to be god-fearing people!"

Vassago scoffs, and the muscle in his jaw feathers. "You'd be surprised how many wolves wear sheep's clothing in this world."

A strangled laugh escapes me, and I fight the urge to shake my head in disbelief. "You're talking about attempted murder, Vassago."

There's a long moment of silence between us, but his low voice sounds louder in the space around us, even amidst the rumbling of the car's engine.

"I know."

# Chapter 27

"Az!" Cole's eyes are wide as saucers as he hurries over to us, immediately inspecting the cuts and scrapes adorning my arms and chest. "What happened!?"

My mouth drops open to answer, but Vassago beats me to it as he places Cole's bag on the counter. "It would seem that your old neighborhood has had a spike in crime, and your house was the latest target."

Cole looks between us before pulling me into a hug, and I wince as the material of his clothes pulls at my cuts just as Vassago disappears around the corner.

"I'm glad you're okay."

My chest tightens, and I nod against his shoulder, ignoring the pain from the pressure of our embrace. "Me too."

"Cole," Vassago says as he appears around the corner once more, "I need to get the glass out of Azura's cuts. Do you mind bringing your duffle bag to your room?"

He instantly releases me, and his wide eyes glance down at the angry red cuts that have started to bleed as he nods. "Shit, yeah. Sorry Az, I didn't know."

Shaking my head, I wave him off and gingerly step over to Vassago's side, eyeing the cloth, tube of cream, and other items in his hands. "They're all superficial. More of a nuisance than anything."

Vassago's lips twitch. "Nuisance or not, even a cut can get infected. Come."

Following Vassago down the long hallway, it's only a mere moment before he leads me into the bathroom, and I stand awkwardly by the sink as he shuts the door, locking it behind him.

Setting the various items on one side of the long counter, he steps over. His hands gingerly wrap around my waist before his grip tightens, and a shrill sound escapes me as he hoists me onto the countertop.

The cold of the stone bites through the thin material of my leggings, and I suppress the shudder that threatens to run through me as he clicks his tongue.

"Keep making sounds like that and they're going to think I'm doing more than just tending to your injuries, Az."

Cold countertop forgotten, my entire body warms as he laughs under his breath, and grasps the cloth from the table, running it under running water for a moment before moving to stand in front of me.

My pulse spikes. "If you tell me to, I will."

He spreads my legs further with his free hand to allow him to get in closer. My heart thrashes in my chest as he meticulously wipes the dried blood from my arms.

The cloth tugs on something in my skin, and I inhale sharply as he freezes and grabs something off the counter. "You're doing so well."

Something gently presses against my skin, and when I can look down, he's wearing a satisfied grin on his face as he holds a pair of tweezers up. Tight in the grip of the pincers is the small shard of glass he plucked from my skin, and he places it on the countertop before wiping the tweezers down.

"One down, two hundred left. Hope you have no plans to sleep."

Vassago pauses, glancing up at me from beneath thick lashes, with pieces of his blonde hair that's fallen forward. "I had no plans to sleep tonight, one way or the other."

The heat in his eyes sends a thrill down my spine, and my gaze falls to his lips.

"Keep looking at me like that, Az, and you'll need a wheelchair tomorrow."

Clearly a glutton for punishment, desire pulses in my core. "Are you threatening me with a good time?"

His lips twitch, and he tugs another shard from my skin as I chew the inside of my cheek.

"What will you do while your brother is on his field trip?" He asks as he continues to pry glass from me every few seconds.

I wince at each twinge of pain. "I think I'll take the time to go through mom's stuff..."

He nods, and moves to lift my shirt overhead now that my arms are clear. "You're welcome to stay with us for the week, too, Az."

My chest tightens, and he focuses on extracting a piece of glass at my hip as I run my fingers through his hair. He glances up at me from beneath thick lashes as another wave of heat washes over me.

"I'd like that at some point, but I think I need the closure."

He hums a quiet agreement, and by the time he's plucked all the shards from my skin, I'm itching to shower with a heavy exhaustion weighing on me.

Vassago gathers the shards, tossing them into the garbage before giving me a long scan from head to toe for any he might have missed. When he doesn't find any, he runs his fingers through my hair, gathering it in a fist at the back of my neck.

"We'll find out who did this, Az. I promise."

The sincerity in his expression has me nodding against his firm grip, and he leans in to press his lips to mine. The ache between my legs is an obvious reminder of what my body's missing, but Vassago pulls back slightly.

"As selfishly as I want to feel you writhing beneath me again, my beloved Azura, you need rest, and that begins with a shower."

I nod, only because I know he's right, and he places another kiss on my forehead before heading out of the bathroom, albeit reluctantly.

By the time the water's hot and I climb in, I'm ready to climb into bed and sleep for years.

But there's still so much left to do.

# Chapter 28

My alarm fills the air and I yawn deeply, swiping my finger across the screen to shut it off. Sun peers in through the window, and I push myself upright as I rub my eyes.

Sleep was elusive for the last few hours of the night, and my mind wandered repeatedly to the funeral, to Cole leaving for his field trip, and to Vassago bringing our case to the school.

I'm not sure that more could happen in one day.

Pacing over to the closet and grabbing the dress Oriana lent me off its hangar, I walk to the bathroom to shower with a numb sort of dread.

Part of me is excited for Cole to get an escape this week, but the more selfish side of me doesn't want to be alone. Especially not after losing mom.

But it's not about what I want.

This is such a huge decision for him to make, and to still want to go after everything...

Tears well in my eyes as I pull my shirt overhead and turning the water on. My arms tremble as I tug the rest of my clothes off and step under the running water.

By the time I'm done, tears have already found their way down my cheeks, and I don't bother wiping the steam from the mirror before pulling on the dress for the funeral.

The soft material hugs my body tight in the waist before flowing down my hips to my thighs, stopping just over my knee, and I release a long sigh.

Whoever Oriana's friend was, I bet she was stunning in this.

After brushing my teeth, I pull open the door only to find Cole standing there waiting, his eyes red and puffy as he stares back at me, and my throat constricts.

"Morning." He whispers, and I step in to wrap my arms around his torso as he shudders.

"We'll get through this, kiddo."

His arms tighten around my shoulders before he releases me from his grip, sniffling. "We need to go soon. Vassago said we have five more minutes."

I frown.

Five minutes?

The funeral isn't for an hour.

Not wanting to question him, I just nod. "Alright, I'll be ready then."

Cole goes into the bathroom, and I hurry back to my room to finish getting ready, which doesn't take long once I've put my hair up, and straightened my bangs.

I'm turning the last corner to the door where Vassago, Cole, Oriana and Seir are standing, and they fall silent as I come into view. My gaze slides to Vassago, and he's looking at me with an expression I can't quite place as Oriana's breath hitches.

When my eyes find hers, I don't miss the tears welling in the corners of her eyes as she gives me a soft smile. "You look beautiful, Azura."

I swallow hard, nodding my head slightly. "I'm certain she looked stunning in it, too."

The tear in her eye escapes as it trails down her cheek, and Seir gently wipes it away with his thumb as she nods. "She most definitely did."

Seir places a tender kiss on the top of her head, and my chest tightens as I watch them head out the door. Taking a deep breath before following them, I see a long limousine waiting in the driveway, and my mouth drops open.

Twisting to look at Vassago, he just winks at me before stepping forward to open the door for me and Cole, as Seir does the same for Oriana on the other side.

Cole climbs in first, and I lean toward Vassago. "A limousine? This is too much!"

His hands move to his chest in shock. "Is it? Here I was thinking it wasn't enough. Oh well... too late now. I suppose all we can do now is just enjoy it."

My mouth snaps shut and I climb inside. He's right.

It's too late now, so all I can do is let it go...

But there's no way this wasn't expensive as hell.

A wave of nausea sends bile into my throat as I consider what my savings will look like after this. Climbing into the limousine, I ease into the seat next to Cole, feeling half dazed as he slides his hand into mine. My eyes slide shut, and I sink into the familiar protectiveness I get with him, and I exhale a ragged breath.

Cole's reaction to the nurse breaking the news in the hospital comes to the forefront of my mind, and my chest tightens painfully as Vassago climbs into the limousine, settling into the seat across from us.

Shifting to get comfortable, his knee rests comfortably against mine, and my eyes snap open at the contact. The feeling is oddly grounding, considering the uncertainty of everything else going on in our lives.

We'll get through this.

My hand squeezes Cole's, as if wordlessly conveying my thoughts, my assurances, my promises, and he gives a single squeeze back as the limousine moves.

I'm lost in my thoughts for most of the drive, and for the most part, everyone stays quiet. A whisper from Oriana here, a remark from Vassago there, but it's mostly a silent drive.

Whether because of the somber feeling hanging in the air or not wanting to diminish the grieving me and Cole are going through, I'm not sure.

I'm thankful for it though.

By the time we pull up to the funeral home, I'm exhausted beyond any reason or logic, and already dreading reopening the wound that had begun to shut since that early morning when she passed.

Vassago climbs out first, and I take his outstretched hand as I tug Cole along with my other. The dark clouds that have rolled over the city over the course of the drive seem fitting for the occasion, and I glance around at the modest dark grey building with crosses etched into the glass of each window and a giant cross erected from the top of the roof. Both doors are propped open, and I take a few steps toward them, with Cole in tow alongside me.

Alright. Let's get this over with.

My feet feel like lead, as if they're weighed down with each step until I'm near the doors, and just as I'm about to step inside, Vassago squeezes past me, murmuring something to the hostess at the front as she glances at each of us with a nod.

"Good morning, Mr. and Ms. Leclair. Everyone, please take a moment to sign in and we will begin shortly once everyone is seated."

The sound of engines fills the air outside as I sign in to the booklet. The notebook is thick-bound, with glossy paper and beautiful designs faded behind each line. Even the pen is an elongated pristine white feather from no bird I've ever seen, and I glide my finger along the silk-like vane before handing it over to Cole.

He's signing in as footsteps fill the air, and a handful of people I don't recognize form a line behind Seir and Oriana.

Is there another funeral happening?

Not wanting to hold everyone up from paying respects to another life lost, I grab Cole's free hand as he sets the quill pen down and lead the way down the hall. At the end, a beautiful set of double doors gives way to a large room with five long rows of benches on each side of the aisle facing a lectern at the front.

Behind it is a colorful display of photos lovingly tucked among bouquets of flowers, and I stare at them in disbelief as we get to the front row. Cole's grip is bruising as we get to our seats, but the way my arm trembles tells me I've likely been squeezing his hand just as hard.

The beautiful white lilies and gladiolus frame each photo, and as I slide into my seat, I soak in each picture with tears welling in my eyes.

The first is one of the few that mom had brought with her after we left Jeffrey. Our first park excursion together with mom when she was off work, while Jeffrey had run to the liquor store one town over because the closest one was closed. Cole's chubby baby cheeks are red from the cold as he smirks at mom, and I'm holding a rock to the camera with a smile that doesn't seem to reach my eyes. Mom's eyes are bright as she looks back at us, and as I stare at the pure joy in her smile, it easily overshadows the lack thereof in mine.

The next photo was from Cole's fifth birthday party at a local bowling alley, with Cole's broad and infectious smile spread from ear to ear as he poses between mom and I.

Mom's eyes look tired, and the lines in her face look more pronounced, but she still smiles at the camera with me, stone-faced and stiff tucked under her arm. Staring back at my younger self, it feels like an out-of-body experience without her being here now.

Because she's gone.

The pillar who kept us moving, kept us afloat, is gone.

Tears flow down my cheeks as I gaze into the distant eyes of my younger self, and I can't help but regret not being more present back then.

Sure, I was going through so much, but I hardly recall anything from the days when these photos were taken. Bits and pieces seem to resurface, but it's hardly more than a hint of what my memory could have been.

The next few photos are ones I'd never seen before, with mom surrounded by people she seems familiar with. Some images were taken in restaurants or at long tables where she's surrounded by people who I can only assume she worked with or were friends with. Some faces reappear in other photos, like a middle-aged blonde woman with kind eyes and bulky necklaces, wearing a flowery shirt in both photos, or the older man with crinkles at the corner of his eyes, white hair, and a toothy grin.

The last photo seated in the center of the rest, and double the size of the others, makes my breath catch in my lungs, and Cole squeezes my hand hard enough that my fingers tingle.

Mom's in her wedding gown, looking more young and energized than I think I'd ever be able to remember her, with blush covered cheeks, a reddish glow to her lips and a beautifully done smokey eye.

Her long brown hair is curled and styled immaculately, with white flowers pinned throughout that tie into her long, flowy dress that hugs her body from her chest to her hips before blooming out into the long train behind her.

The ornate stitching in the train of her dress looks like flower petals as it curls around her before reaching the floor, and I stare at her in all her glory as tears drop to my chest, soaking into my skin.

She gave everything to us.

My breath hitches again, and I stare at the version of my mom that existed before Jeffrey, before me, and before Cole.

The woman who risked a life of jail to protect her children, and stole us away to a place he'd never find us.

She deserved so much more.

A cough fills the air right behind us, and I'm pulled back to the present, turning my head to glance at rows of people with puffy eyes and sniffling noses, all donned in black. It's not until I recognize the blonde woman from the photos that my heart breaks anew.

Some part of me expected it to just be the five of us.

I don't even know how Vassago got word to the people mom knew to tell them of the funeral.

At the thought, my eyes gravitate to where he sits beside me, seeing him gazing at the photos, lost in his own distant thoughts until I slide my palm into his, and his attention turns to me.

Tracking the tear stains on my cheek, he searches my face and gives my hand a gentle squeeze.

"Thank you for this." My voice is hardly more than a whisper, but I might as well have yelled it with how loud it felt in the air between us as he inclines his head once.

He opens his mouth to speak as Father Arrenault steps up to us, giving Oriana and Seir a sidelong glance from where they sit next to Cole before reaching over to take my hand.

Even mourning the loss of mom isn't enough to stop the urge to jerk my hand away.

"My dear child," his calloused hands scrape against my knuckles, and he pats the back of my hand before doing the same to Cole. "Surely your mother is watching over you both. May the Lord bless you."

Cole murmurs something into my ear, but it's too low for me to understand, and I feel my throat tighten as Vassago gets up to stand behind the lectern.

Seeing him stand before the incredibly beautiful display feels surreal, and part of me knows that if mom is looking down at us, that she would have loved Vassago for doing all of this.

He clasps his hands on top of the lectern, and his grey irises scan over the rows of seats. "Family and friends of Mrs. Leclair. We gather here today to mourn the loss of a pillar in our community and our family. Though Mrs. Elisa Leclair is gone, each of you will keep her memory alive. In the memories you made, the futures you built, and the paths you chose together. I'm proud to have the honor of inviting her daughter, the lovely Azura Leclair, to commemorate Elisa's life."

My hand trembles as Cole releases it, and I unsteadily make my way to where Vassago stands, feeling his hand gravitate to the small of my back before he moves his seat once more.

"Thank you everyone, for being here today to mourn the loss of an incredible woman, mother, and friend, while also celebrating her life with us."

My gaze surveys the now filled room of teary-eyed people, and the lump in my throat grows as my mind blanks on the eulogy I'd absently practiced in my head over the past few days. "It's hard to believe she had this many friends."

My huff of laughter is echoed throughout the room, and a rogue tear falls down my cheek as I blow out a breath. "I won't stand here and pretend I knew her better than the rest of you did, because I think that would do her a disservice. The Elisa Leclair I knew was a fierce, strong and resilient woman who would do anything for Cole and me. Even if that meant spending her waking hours working herself to the bone just to make ends meet."

The blonde woman covers her mouth and nose with a napkin as tears pour down her cheeks, and I blink away tears of my own. "She gave everything to build a life for the three of us, but she never forgot a birthday, a choir recital, a practice or a milestone moment. She was our light in the dark, and every day that I'm alive, I will be thankful for the woman she was."

A handful of people clap as a man from the front row steps forward to the lectern. When I return to my seat, I glance over the crowd and the five men scattered across the back of the room wearing white suits and dark shades that stand out like sore thumbs.

By the time I've sunk into the seat beside Cole, I exhale a ragged breath and Cole's hand slides into mine once more, giving my hand a tense squeeze.

After a few more speeches are done, Vassago steps up to the front once more, looking more somber than I'd seen him before this event started.

"Friends and family of the Leclairs, our partners here at the funeral home will start the procession to the cemetery shortly. It isn't a far distance, and per Mrs. Elise Leclair's will, Father Arrenault will perform rites of committal."

The next few minutes are a blur as we load into the limousine, and Cole keeps his arm firmly locked in mine for the whole drive. My mind keeps rounding back to the display, with mom's youthful, energized visage burned into my thoughts the entire way there.

Vassago's been quiet for the duration of the ride, and even Seir and Oriana have stayed oddly silent even as we unload from the vehicle, making the short walk to the burial site.

White lilies and gladiolus surround the beautifully engraved white casket on all sides, with elegant golden symbols etched over the surface that I don't recognize from any of the pictures we looked at together.

Seir and Oriana are the first to reach the few chairs immediately in front of the burial site, and I take a seat beside them as Vassago sits beside Cole to my right.

The same youthful wedding photo sits on a tall easel surrounded by flowers, and Father Arrenault steps over to the lectern beside it, his eyes narrowing as they trail over the casket.

Clearly he doesn't approve of the style, but he says nothing as others file in and surround us from all sides. It takes a few minutes for him to get started, and I'm lost in thought as he recites prayers that I somehow still remember from my youth.

My mind wanders as time goes on, and his readings meld into the sound of sniffling from the crowd behind us as Cole gives my hand a squeeze. When I glance over at him, seeing his puffy, bloodshot eyes gazing back at me, the knot in my stomach grows, and I tug his arm closer, leaning the side of my head against his shoulder as Father Arrenault gives final blessings over mom's burial site.

"Into your hands, Father, we commend our sister Elisa Leclair, that, together, with all who have died in Christ, she may rise with Him on the last day. May He grant eternal rest unto her, O Lord, and let His perpetual light shine upon her. May she rest in peace. Amen."

Vassago steps to the lectern, his soft gaze focused on me as he addresses everyone. "We will now lower the casket. Thank you to everyone paying respects today to Mrs. Elisa Leclair. Please be safe on your way home."

The crowd murmurs, and I watch as a handful of men in suits move to lower the casket down before turning to look at the others. A few people are leaving the area, heading back to their cars as others say goodbye to one another as others hug or murmur in small groups. The five men in white suits still stand around the back of the group like statues, their shades so dark that it's nearly impossible to see their eyes, and I turn back to the front.

*Maybe funeral security?*

*Is that a thing?*

The casket starts to lower, and I release a deep sigh as I start to think forward to the rest of the day. Papers being served, Cole's field trip, and I still need to go to work this afternoon.

*Lord help me.*

# Chapter 29

Pulling into the parking lot of Blackwell's office, my stomach turns uncomfortably. Saying goodbye to Cole and Vassago was hard enough, but watching them both walk into Rennensberg, knowing I won't see either of them for a week?

It felt like my heart was breaking into two... Well... More like three.

I know I could have stayed with them while Cole is gone, but I figured this was a good time for me to go through mom's things, and get used to her not being around anymore.

Even as heart shattering as it is to consider.

My footsteps are heavy as I walk to the front door, and wonder how Mr. Humphrey will look when Vassago serves the papers to him.

How long would it be until Blackwell gets a call from the school? Hours? Days? Weeks?

Pushing past the doorway to the desk, I catch sight of Blackwell standing beside it, staring at his phone with a frown.

Ah, make that minutes, actually.

He glances up at me before sliding his phone into the pocket of his dress pants and clears his throat.

"Azura. Good to see you."

I incline my head once. "Hi."

There's an awkward moment of silence before he steps aside, motioning for me to sit down. "I heard about your mother. I'm sorry for your loss."

He... sorry? Has hell frozen over?

Resisting the urge to look at the window to see if the sky is falling, I walk past him to my seat. "Thank you."

"I didn't think you'd be in. Are you staying the entire afternoon?"

I nod. "Yes. I may need to step out to take one call from contractors at the house to replace the window by the front door, but otherwise, I don't expect any interruptions."

The look on his face is a mixture of hesitancy and wariness as he nods. "Right. Well, welcome back. I'll be in my office. You can send my eleven o'clock in when he gets here."

He disappears into his office, and I exhale a ragged breath of relief. Of all the days for him to be more human, thank God today is the day.

A few hours go by, and I'm grabbing a file from the cabinet when the door chime fills the air.

"Just a minute, please."

Footsteps grow closer, halting a few feet away, and I roll a few inches back to my desk and glance up at the man standing before me. He's probably only a couple inches taller than me, with a long scar along his right cheek, but he's dressed in an expensive-looking suit, with a look on his face that appears outwardly polite, but something about it sends a shiver of dread down my spine.

"Your name, please?"

"Gerald Smithson."

The dread proves to be right as I nod once at the board member of Rennensberg High School, and move to open the door.

It takes all my focus to keep one foot in front of the other as I hold the door open for him. "Mr. Blackwell will see you now, Mr. Smithson. Thank you."

Closing the door behind him, my heart is in my throat as I ease down into my seat once more.

Does he know?

Is he telling Blackwell right now?

Bile rises in my throat, and I take a centering breath as my phone buzzes.

**Vassago:** Would you hate me if I stopped by the house today to check on the contractors?

My lips twitch. Of course he did.

**Azura:** Not a chance. It's a relief, actually. I expected that I would have to step away, but Blackwell's eleven o'clock appointment may be the end of my career.

Vassago reads the message instantly, but a long moment passes before he responds, and I feel close to vomiting while I wait.

**Vassago:** Whatever happens, just remember, just because we did the right thing, doesn't mean it will be easy.

Exhaling a deep breath, I nod absently as I type out a response.

**Azura:** Trying to remember, but feel free to remind me later.

Movement in Blackwell's office sounds out, and I slide my phone into my purse before flipping through a file absently. The door to his office opens, and both men walk out, chuckling as they head out the door to the parking lot.

There's no way I'll keep my job through this.

I'm mentally sorting through which places I could submit a resume to when the door chime sounds out again, and Blackwell walks inside.

"Azura! Have you eaten today?"

Blinking at him, I shake my head. "No, sir."

Blackwell's face lights up, and he puts both hands in the air. "Well! I know just the place. I'll order. Any allergies?"

Shaking my head again, it takes a conscious effort to school my features. "No allergies here."

He snaps his fingers once, and hurries into his office excitedly, leaving me staring at the empty doorway in a state of shock.

*Who is this and what the hell have they done with Blackwell?*

By the time I'm off work, I don't know what to think about his sudden change in demeanor. He was cheerful all day, even saying goodbye and telling me to drive safely when I was leaving for the afternoon.

Pulling onto Dartmouth Street, I'm glancing around nervously for the white car with tinted windows before pulling into the driveway. With no sign of trouble, I get out and take the dreaded steps to the newly replaced door. The repairs Vassago helped coordinate look almost invisible as I unlock it, glancing over my shoulder every few seconds until I'm inside, heaving a sigh of relief as I slide the bolt in place, and survey the hall.

The room smells of fresh paint, and not a shard of glass remains to be seen as I walk to the couch, glancing down at where I'd been hiding as my mind struggles to keep memory from the present.

Phone buzzing, I'm snapped from my reverie as I look at the text.

**Cole:** Bus is heading out now. Text you later, Az.

**Azura:** Love ya kiddo.

Walking over to my bedroom, I heave a sigh of relief before peeling off the dress Oriana lent me, and climbing into the shower. The heat washes away the stress, anxieties and the rest of my nerves of the day. By the time I'm done, I'm left with an exhaustion that seems to have worn me down to the bone.

Releasing a deep sigh, I turn the water off and climb out of the shower, toweling myself dry as my phone vibrates on the counter. When I unlock it, I frown at the ID showing an unknown number and the text preview being a link to some website about demons.

*Not this shit again.*

Rolling my eyes, I block the number and delete the text before pulling on an oversized t-shirt when my phone vibrates again.

**Vassago:** Rennensberg High School officially has representation.

My heart drops to the bottom of my stomach like a bag of rocks.

**Azura:** Who?

**Vassago:** I'll give you one guess.

**Azura:** Fuck.

**Vassago:** It's being filed to state court. They have a few weeks to respond, but it has begun.

**Azura:** That's not terrifying at all.

**Vassago:** What is there to be afraid of?

**Azura:** Everything. I'm hanging on by a thread.

**Vassago:** It will be fine, Az. Just try to relax tonight.

Walking to the front room, I inspect the couch closely for glass, relieved when there's none, and I sit back comfortably, turning the television on to a comedy channel.

After an hour, my eyes weigh heavily, and each blink feels like I'm fighting against the world, so I turn the power button off and stumble to the room.

Flopping into the soft comfort of my bed, I release a deep breath, feeling myself sink into the material as sleep claims me.

# Chapter 30

"Azura, my office, please."

My heart thumps steadily as I pace into Blackwell's office, and pause a foot from the door as he clasps his hands together.

"Yes, sir?"

His brow raises. "Are we just going to pretend like you didn't sue Rennensberg?"

I swallow, shaking my head. "No, sir. It just hadn't come up."

He rolls his eyes and pushes to his feet. "Well, consider it 'up' now. Working together is officially a conflict of interest, and effective immediately, you're on an unpaid administrative leave for the foreseeable future."

I nod once, feeling tears well in the corners of my eyes, even though I knew it was coming.

"Yes, sir."

I turn to leave, but Blackwell's voice halts me in place. "You'd do well to stay away from that attorney, Azura. I know you're ignorant of his practices, but stay away from him."

I frown, clearing my throat. "Have a good day, Mr. Blackwell."

My feet carry me from the office faster than I ever thought possible, and a rogue tear trails down my cheek as I climb into my car.

Even though I knew where this was going to go in the end, it didn't lessen the sting. Reaching into the center console, I pull out a copy of my resume that I'd printed off a few months prior, and I drop off resumes at the only two places in town currently hiring on the way home.

Our local pet rescue, and our library.

I take an extra two hours to get home with dropping off applications, but I'm still home by lunchtime, and with nothing to keep myself busy, I sit down in front of my computer, sorting through local places hiring.

After an eternal thirty minutes of searching, I pull out my phone and go to my messages.

**Azura:** Blackwell officially put me on unpaid leave today.

**Vassago:** I'm so sorry, Az. Can't say I'm surprised beyond that he waited until the morning to do it.

**Azura:** Yeah, and he was in a scarily good mood yesterday.

**Vassago:** How out of character?

I huff a laugh as I type out my answer.

**Azura:** I expected him to be his normal stone faced self, but he was actually really... human?

**Vassago:** Nightmare fuel.

I continue to scroll through job postings, seeing the only available options are hours away, which won't work for where we live right now. Keywords being right and now, because with how things are going, we'll have to move somewhere more affordable in the future.

Sighing in resignation, I lean back as an engine hums outside for a long moment, and I'm hanging by a thread, waiting to hear if I should duck and cover before the sound grows more faint.

Releasing the breath I'd been holding, I hear the chime of a notification come through and quickly flick over to it, only to see an email from someone named "Lord's Messenger."

I roll my eyes. *How cliché.*

Opening the email out of pure curiosity, I see a link to a well known streaming website. Accompanying the link is the same username and a private viewing passcode.

I frown.

Not wanting to click a random link, I go to my browser and type in the streaming website before searching for the username, and my heart drops when I see Lord's Messenger is live-streaming by invite only.

Butterflies soar chaotically in my stomach as I click on the "Watch now" button, and type the private viewing passcode in with trembling hands.

The stream displays two camera views of two areas, and I stare with wide eyes at the familiar face of the medic who had grabbed my arm roughly and the cop who had shoved me to the ground. They're both standing in the middle of a room glancing around nervously as if they're terrified.

Who the hell sent me this?

A message pops up in the chat, and the hair on the back of my neck stands up.

**Lord's Messenger:** Are you finally ready to open your eyes and see?

I say nothing as the officer shoves the paramedic angrily, but they both jolt in the same direction to something or someone off-screen, and my pulse spikes as they take a step back.

There's no audio, but I can see them both take another healthy step back before the officer breathes hard. He looks wildly between the paramedic and whatever or whoever else is in the room before tearing his uniform off, leaving only his pants on as the medic places a palm out to whoever is with them.

I'm not a lip-reader by any means, but even with the mediocre quality video, it's clear as day when he says "please stop," repeatedly.

Please stop what, though?

I frown as the officer suddenly leans back, and his skin blisters as if someone boiled him alive before my eyes. The medic flinches as the boils burst, splattering him with liquid before the officer's skin sloughs off.

Caught between horror and morbid curiosity, I can't tear my eyes away from the screen as the officer's skin gives way to bare muscle and broken blood vessels that turn black like char.

The cop's mouth is open, but he's since stopped moving, even though his body continues to burn or disintegrate without a single flame taken to it.

The medic keels over and vomits before dropping to his knees, placing his palms out in surrender before scrambling backward with wide eyes.

Step by step, the missing puzzle piece comes into view, and all the oxygen feels like someone sucked it from the room as I watch Vassago stride confidently toward the medic, ignoring the body beside him that is little more than charcoal.

The medic vomits again before his face contorts into rage, and he shouts something at Vassago with his lip curled into a snarl.

I'm still trying to work through the lip-reading of what he shouted when Vassago laughs, turning as if he's about to walk away before pausing.

It's like watching a train wreck as he murmurs something to the medic, and his eyes remain glued to the man before him, watching his skin turn red. The medic palms his face with wild eyes, and my hand covers my mouth in horror as his mouth drops open to scream.

"Vassago..."

My voice is hardly more than a whisper as tears fall from my eyes, and I watch the man I thought I knew flick his wrist suddenly as the medic's neck snaps.

**Lord's Messenger:** Are your eyes open?

*This can't be real.*

*Vassago would never...*

Suddenly, his words in the car send my mind into a whirlwind of confusion.

*Is he a magic wielder? A magic wielder and he's a murderer?*

*Oh god, he's a murderer.*

The live stream ends abruptly, and I close out of the browser before shutting my laptop.

*What should I do?*

*What the hell do I do?*

He just murdered two people. He murdered two people and someone knew enough to livestream it.

*Why didn't they record it and expose him?*

*Are they scared of him? Of what he'll do to them?*

*What would he do to me?*

*Oh, god.*

A loud knock at the front door has me nearly jump out of my skin, and I curse myself for leaving a light on before I creep over to the hallway. Footsteps recede down the patio steps, and I sink down the wall of my bedroom, out of view of any windows or doors as an engine starts on the street.

My eyes squeeze shut as I wait patiently for the rumble to fade into the distance, exhaling a ragged breath before flipping the lights off.

*Worse comes to worst, I can say I was sleeping.*

*I was sleeping, and I didn't hear anyone knock. That happens right?*

Not wanting to sleep in my bed, I walk quietly to mom's room, locking the door behind me before tossing stuff off her bed, and crawling under the covers.

*What if it was a faked video? A falsified live-stream? Curated just to drive a wedge between us and break the trust we've built?*

The mental image of both men boiling alive flashes through my mind, and I blow out a tense breath.

*What if it isn't?*

Pulling my phone out, I unlock the screen to see a missed text from Vassago, but nothing from Cole, so I open his messages.

**Azura:** You safe, kiddo? Hope you're having fun. Miss you lots.

My mind is a jumbled mess for hours, and by the time sleep finally finds me, it's restless. I'm woken up by every sound, every car driving by, and every creak in the house until exhaustion finally takes its toll, and darkness claims me.

# Chapter 31

"I'm sorry, Ms. Leclair. I don't think you'd be a good fit for this company and our values here."

My brows pinch together as I stare at the owner of the pet rescue company after a lengthy interview.

"May I ask why?"

The owner, an older man with a white beard and balding crown, wrings his hands together before his eyes shift to the window. "Well, you see, there's a certain reputation you have around town for not, well, not living by His teachings, and here at Rennensberg Rescue, we don't take kindly to people dragging His name through the mud."

My mouth drops open, but he just waves me off dismissively. "I won't change my mind now, kid. Best be going if you know what's good for you."

I push to my feet in a huff before hurrying to the parking lot and glance at the time.

*Shit.* I've got forty-five minutes to get to the library.

My sleep-deprived mind has been a chaotic mess all day, and even though I'm sure I didn't ace my interview with Rennensberg Rescue, I have already started to put the pieces together as to why they decided against hiring me.

Humphrey had said his threat loud and clear early on, and I'm nearly certain that's where the denial came from.

The live-stream pops into my mind once again, and I shove it away from my attention with force.

*Nope.* If I'm going to be a productive member of society, it'll be without thinking of whatever that was. I have bigger problems.

The drive to the library is uneventful, and by the time I've pulled into the parking lot, I'm two minutes late. Hurrying through the doors, I come to a stop in front of the librarian's desk. The middle-aged woman glances up before fully turning her head to me.

"How can I help you?"

Fighting to not sound like I'm in the worst shape of my life, I give her a sweet smile. "Azura Leclair. I have an interview scheduled."

The librarian glances at the clock with a raised brow, but pushes to her feet, anyway. "Come with me." She leads me to another side room and motions for me to go inside. "Wait here one moment, please."

I slide into the seat as she closes the door, and I'm finally able to catch my breath for a few minutes while I wait. A few more minutes go by, and I look around the minimalistic room, with only the pencils and paper on the side of the table.

My mind gravitates to Vassago, but I quickly shove him out of my thoughts before moving onto Cole, and I pull out my phone to see he still hasn't reached out.

Frowning, I open his messages again.

**Azura:** Hey, are you okay?

When he doesn't read the message, I dial his number and let it ring until his answering machine picks up.

The door opens to the room, and I drop the phone to my lap as the librarian steps inside.

"Hi Ms. Leclair. I'm sorry to have to do this, but we're going to have to cancel your interview. Because of your recent lawsuit against Rennensberg High School and in the best interest of our town, we are going to pursue other candidates at this time."

I blink at her, still in shock that I've been outwardly denied twice.

"Thank you." I murmur before pushing to my feet and exiting the room, feeling tears stain my cheeks as I hurry to the car.

The moment I close the door, my anger rises to the surface and I grip the handle tight as I scream. My chest heaves, and my forehead drops to the steering wheel as tears pour from my eyes.

If I don't find something soon, I won't be able to support both of us, and Seir and Oriana will have to keep Cole permanently. My eyes squeeze shut, and I shudder as a sob crawls out of my throat.

*Maybe I can find something out of town?*

*We could get a fresh start.*

Pulling out my phone, I go to Cole's messages and see all of mine unread as a pit forms in my stomach.

*Why isn't he responding?*

Opening my email, I file through to the email from the school with the details of the field trip before keying in the address into my GPS.

*Am I really about to go track down Cole because he isn't answering me?*

My mind replays what happened to the cop and medic and my resolve solidifies as I turn the engine on.

Best-case scenario, he lost his phone, and I'm a crazy big sister.

Worst-case scenario... I'll cross that bridge when I get to it.

I'm about to put the car into drive when I get another email, and dread settles into my gut as I stare at the name Lord's Messenger in the preview before it disappears.

My heart leaps into my throat, and I tab over to open it.

**Lord's Messenger:** Your eyes are open, but you still have much to learn... So learn you must.

The body of the email has fifty links to different websites, but in each URL, Vassago's name is spelled in different ways. I swallow hard, staring at them like they'll magically disappear at any moment.

The parking lot is empty around me as I tab to my browser and search for his name.

The first three results are for Gloam Legal, which doesn't come as a surprise, but as I scroll down, the results are all the same. Hundreds of websites describing one Vassago, the Prince of Hell.

I scroll through the first page, seeing reference to Goetic demons in the Lesser Key of Solomon. Summoning instructions by each of their names–that I'm certain have to be made up–sends my mind into a spiral.

*This can't be legit.*

I close out of it and tab back to my GPS, setting my phone on the stand as my mind races.

*It has to be a coincidence.*

*Someone who just got too carried away with naming their kids.*

*That happens right?*

I get lightheaded and take a centering breath.

*Okay. It's fine. It's fine. I'll go home, tomorrow I'll drive to the camp, make sure Cole's okay, and then we'll sort the rest out.*

Putting the car in drive, I make my way back home feeling like my entire world has shifted on its axis.

And perhaps it has.

# Chapter 32

My phone vibrates, and I unlock my screen to see another message from Vassago, and my heart feels like it's being torn to shreds.

I hate ignoring him, but with my mind so focused on Cole's lack of response and everything else going on, I haven't been able to bring myself to respond without thinking about that damn stream.

It's been an hour since I got home, and I've sat on my bedroom floor, staring at the wall, waiting for Cole to respond to my messages, or even read them.

I called him twice when I got home, and both calls went to voicemail, which is now full. So all I can do now is wait.

My phone buzzes again, and I open Vassago's messages.

**Vassago:** Blackwell and Rennensberg have agreed to start trial as early as next week. I'll pencil you in for Monday. We can go over what to expect with this being a state court case.

**Vassago:** Assuming your interview went as suspected?

**Vassago:** T-Minus two hours before I send search and rescue to find you.

I'm fully aware the last message is meant to be funny, but after seeing what I have, all I hear is the unspoken threat behind his words. I stare at his message for a long moment before typing out my response.

**Azura:** Both interviews done. No offers. Next week sounds good... Can we push it to Tuesday?

I'm fully aware one day will not do much, but one more day is a full twenty-four hours for me to process what the hell I saw and figure out how I can ask him without sounding insane.

He reads it instantly and starts typing as my heart feels like it could leap out of my throat.

**Vassago:** With good reason, I could argue it to be later in the week. Do you have conflicts or is there something you're not telling me?

My heart pounds at his direct question that seems far too pointed for him to be oblivious, but I blow out a breath.

**Azura:** Cole hasn't responded to my messages since leaving, and he hasn't answered any of my calls. I'm just worried.

**Vassago:** That's odd. Do you want me to check on him?

**Azura:** No, it's fine. He probably lost his phone. I'll give it another day.

He reads the message but says nothing, and I walk over to the bathroom, popping two of mom's all-natural extra strength sleeping aids into my mouth and I wash them down with a gulp of tap water.

If I'm going to go search for Cole tomorrow, I'm going to need all the rest I can get...

After moving clothes and other items off mom's bed, I slide under the plush comforter, and my eyes squeeze shut. I lay there for a long while, waiting for sleep to finally claim me. Seconds, minutes, even hours go by, and yet I lay there awake, with my thoughts centered on what will happen when I go to see Cole tomorrow.

I've thought through every scenario of what I need to do tomorrow, with all of them resulting in Cole just having lost his phone or it having broken.

But each time, that small voice in the back of my mind asks, "but what if that's not what happened?"

By the time my restlessness pushes me to action, it's pitch black in the house, and my exhaustion is at its peak. I release a long sigh, and my eyes flutter open to the shadows dancing against the ceiling.

*Fuck it.*

*I don't care if it's two AM. I'm going to get my baby brother.*

Kicking the blankets off, I swing my legs off the bed and sit up, feeling lightheaded and woozy before standing. It takes three times as long to dress, but I'm at least half lucid by the time I get to the door, with car keys in hand.

I'm fully aware that I'm beyond exhausted and not in any state to be doing this, but I can't wait any longer.

Cole wouldn't wait if roles were reversed.

Another sinking note of anxiety and dread settles in my stomach as I walk to the car, having to focus twice as hard on walking properly just to get to the driver's side door.

Climbing into the seat, I lock the doors and GPS to the campsite, seeing a fifty-minute drive with no traffic, and I take a deep breath. I'm extra cautious as I back out before starting the long journey.

I swear to God if he's not okay, I will burn this world to the ground and everyone with it.

# Chapter 33

The road to the campsite is dark and narrow, and according to the GPS, it's less than a five-minute walk from the main highway, so I pull the car over into a small maintenance entrance and leave the keys inside the unlocked cabin before treading the rest of the path on foot.

Each step through the forest is unsteady thanks to the sleep aids I'd taken, and the minimal light from the half moon that isn't helping guide my way at all. I stay parallel to the small path to the campsite, keeping myself low as I make my way deeper.

My phone buzzes in my pocket just as voices carry on the air from a distance, and I'm instantly on alert, crouching down as the trees give way to buildings only fifty feet ahead.

I spot two older men sitting by the back door of what looks to be a worn down building as they pass a cigarette between one another as they idly chatter.

Butterflies soar inside my body as I realize I just drove nearly an hour while impaired to spy on camp workers to find my brother.

*This is crazy.*

*There's no way I won't look insane if anyone finds me.*

The men both stand, and I duck behind a tree, watching as one steps on the remnants of his cigarette, and they both head inside with the door loudly slamming shut behind them.

*Okay, think Az.*

*Cole's gotta be around here somewhere...*

Another thud sounds out somewhere beyond the building, and my heart is in my throat as I cautiously place each step, quietly making my way through the forest until I finally spot another smaller building just beyond the first.

Footsteps fill the air once more, and I crouch down just as a young girl carries a broom around the corner. Her cheeks are sunken in, her hair is matted to shit, and her skin is arguably covered with more dirt than the ground I stand on.

I watch in horror as the pit in my stomach grows.

She hauls the long broom to the door, wincing as she steps off the dirt and onto the wooden panels before closing the door behind her.

*God. Please don't tell me that was what I think it was.*

Child labor is illegal in most states before the age of fourteen, but she looked to be no older than ten.

A long moment passes, and I continue along the edge of the forest line, staying hidden as I survey the rest of the campsite. After passing by three more buildings, I'm about to move past what I assumed were the run down remains of a building when a clatter echoes into the air.

A faint whimper breaks the silence as I watch two men tug another young girl toward the ruined building with horror.

"I don't think this one is ready, Jeff."

The shorter man–Jeff–shrugs as they pull her to a kitchen area where a large rug covers the floor, and one man holds the girl by the hair as the other yanks the carpet back.

"Good thing you're not paid to do the thinking, then." Jeff turns to the taller man and leans in, giving me a clear view of his face as my blood runs cold. "You've got three minutes to get done thinking before she's presented to him and sanctified. When we get through that tunnel, you best have a rational mind."

It's been years since I laid eyes on the man who helped conceive Cole and me, but as I stare at him, the familiar fear-laced rage boils to the surface as if no time has passed at all.

Years of drinking have made his skin uneven, wrinkled with deep frown lines, and the hardness in his expression hasn't softened any. It's not until he turns away from the taller man that my trance finally breaks, and he moves to an exposed spot on the floor where the carpet looks to have been moved.

Lines in the shape of a rectangle mark the ground, breaking the evenness of the grains of the wooden flooring as the realization hits me.

*A hidden entrance.*

The taller man hoists the door open, holding it for Jeffrey as he tugs the girl along with him before the door eases shut.

*Sanctified?*

*If they're bringing her there, maybe Cole is there too?*

I glance around at the buildings once more, spotting two more that I've yet to take a look at, and my palms grow slick with sweat.

The buildings have no windows, so I'd be going inside and risking getting caught whereas if I go into the tunnel, I might also get caught, but maybe I'll find Cole there with any other kids they brought.

My gaze shifts from the door to the buildings, and I'm about to go inspect the final two when the hidden door opens once more.

Ducking down into cover, I watch as the taller man saunters to the nearest building, muttering to himself. "He can bring her himself then, if I'm such a pain."

*If I'm going to go into the tunnel, it's better now than never.*

The man disappears around the corner, and I hurry to the door, still half crouched as my heart threatens to beat out of my chest. Within seconds, I've slipped into the dark underground passage, and the musty, earthy scent invades my senses as I spot a light in the distance.

Each step toward it sends a fresh wave of adrenaline through my veins, and by the time I've gotten to the large, dimly lit room with several pillars in the center. The room is empty, but I spot a small entryway with stairs going down off to the left.

Spotting a few more doorways to tunnels, I suck in a breath and go with my gut. Quiet murmuring carries in the air, and I keep to the edge of the room before walking down another set of stairs where the voices seem to be collected.

The stairs give way to a short tunnel, and I get to the entrance of a large room with similar pillars in the center. The murmuring gets louder with each step, and it's almost in a rhythm as my gaze lands on what might just be the second most horrifying sight I've ever laid eyes on.

The young girl from earlier kneels in the center of a circle of pillars with five masked men surrounding her on all sides, and a sixth directly behind her.

Candles line the circle of pillars, with symbols drawn around them in red, and the young girl in the middle of the circle groans as her head tilts back. Her hair shifts with the movement, exposing the long wound spanning from her shoulder to her opposite hip.

She's bruised, battered and bleeding out with what I can only assume are pieces of her own organs jutting from her abdomen.

The chanting continues, and bile rises in my throat as blood pools around her. She chokes as blood splatters from her mouth, and her organs push out of the wound from the pressure as the contents of my stomach threaten to come up.

I debate calling the police, but if I do, they'll think I'm crazy.

Adrenaline pumps through my veins, and I pull out my phone to Vassago's messages.

*If there's one person who would believe me, it would be him.*

The screen is blindingly bright in the shadows of the tunnel, and I squint against it.

**Vassago:** We found out who the shooter was. Your father isn't dead, Az.

My gut twists, and I glance up to the room as a man in the ring and I lock eyes.

*Shit.*

Adrenaline rages in my body as I whirl around, only to come face to face with the tormentor of my past–my father.

He's so close that I'm able to see each stubble of hair on his chin, the faded scar on his temple that spans down to his cheek and the hard look in his eyes before something collides with the back of my skull, and the world suddenly goes dark.

# Chapter 34

"... Maybe."

Pain radiates from the back of my head, and I wince as the throbbing sends echoes lancing down my neck.

"... St. Michael, hear my pleas..."

My ears hear the words being murmured in a hush around me, but it's not until my eyes peel open that I realize where they're coming from. The bars of the tiny, cell-like space I'm in come into my view.

But my small prison isn't the only one.

They lined the room with them, all stacked on one another, and each is large enough to fit one adult or two children, which looks to be exactly what these people have done.

My gaze scans along the walls, and I count at least six children in the first row, which means there's easily enough room to confine anywhere upwards of forty children in this building alone.

I glance around for my phone, and when it's not anywhere to be found, I know full well that I must have dropped it in the tunnel, which means it's still there, or they took it.

Dread coils in my stomach as I scan through everyone I can see, and Cole isn't there.

*Could he be above me?*

*In a different building?*

Most of the children are sleeping or appear to be, and my eyes gravitate to the ones praying before I spot the others. I notice two kids standing out among a couple who are zoned out, their eyes distant.

They're standing on opposite sides of the bars that barricade them from one another, talking quietly with cautious eyes darting from side to side.

It's not until the further boy makes eye contact with me, and they both pause with their faces paling before turning away.

"Wait!"

I hurry to the bars of my prison, and both look at me warily as my mind registers the jacket the boy is wearing matches the jacket Cole was wearing when he left.

"That," I point to him and squeeze myself to the bars, "Where did you get that?"

The two young teens glance at one another before he responds. "My friend gave it to me."

With each passing second, I feel like I'm teetering on the edge of desperation and insanity as I nod. "Cole?"

The kid's eyes widen. "Yeah, how did you know?"

*If he was here to give them his jacket, he might still be safe.*

"Where is he?"

The two kids glance at one another again, and I'm about to ask again when the door bursts open, and Jeffrey saunters into the room.

"Finally awake are we?"

He steps in front of the cage, and I'm too slow to back up as his hand snaps between the bars, weaving into the hair at the nape of my neck before jerking my face into the bars.

"Where the hell did you come from, huh?"

When I don't answer, he pulls my head back and slams my face against them again.

"Who the fuck sent you, bitch?"

Pain radiates through my skull, and my eyes squeeze shut.

*If I can just hold out long enough to find Cole...*

He suddenly releases my hair with force before moving into the center of the room, and all the children seem to gravitate away from the bars of their confinement as his beady eyes level with mine.

"Next time I come in here, you better have a fucking answer for me." He glances at another man by the door before tilting his head toward my cage. "Bring the kid. We'll be back at dusk."

My eyes drop to see a defeated and distant-eyed Anna being hauled over to the door. Jeffrey unlocks the padlock with the twist of a key, and when the man pushes Anna roughly, I grab her before she loses her balance entirely.

The men stalk out of the room, and I spin Anna around to look at her.

"Anna." Her eyes stay distant, and I jostle her shoulders. "Anna, it's me, Az. Where is Cole?"

She seems to snap slightly out of it as her gaze finally focuses on me, and it's a few tortuously long seconds before she shakes her head ever so slightly.

"I don't know."

I frown. "What do you mean, you don't know?"

"Someone moved him into a separate building from the one I was in. He was doing a lot of chores, but I never saw him after."

*Chores.*

*Oh, thank god.*

*There's still a chance he's okay.*

I'm fully aware that after seeing what I did earlier, that my line of thought is selfish, but I came here for Cole, and I'll be damned if I don't find him and get him out before something happens to me.

"Anna," I murmur, and her dull eyes flick to me lazily. "What are they doing here?"

She stares at me for a long moment, before looking at the door with a look that's horrifyingly close to longing, and I almost dread the answer as she opens her mouth to speak.

"Miracles."

# Chapter 35

It's been hours since they left a battered and bruised Anna in the cell with me.

Through all that time, she's rambled about these men being saviors. She muttered to herself broken and incoherent prayers for God to save her soul and deliver everyone from evil. Any time I've asked her what she means by it, she just tells me that miracles happen here.

The sun shafts peering through cracks in the wooden log walls have gradually disappeared, throwing most of the room into shadow where the single dim yellow light in the center of the room can't reach.

The stench, which was once overwhelmingly putrid, has now become normal, and outside of the times where one of the kids uses the washroom in their cage, it's been manageable.

I only threw up four times, and dry heaved six more.

That said, I wasn't prepared when the children above our confined quarters kicked the urine or shit over the edge. It only took one time to get splattered for me to stay as far away from the edge as possible.

Distant footsteps carry in the air as they grow closer, and the hushed prayers from various cells quiets down just as the door pushes open, and Jeffrey takes two heavy steps inside with the tall man and another trailing close behind.

"Well, well, well." Jeffrey grins with a curl of his upper lip, surveying the room closely. "Guess we'll have to pick someone at random. Wonder who that'll be."

His gaze lands on Anna, and I tug her behind me protectively.

*No, this was the person Cole repeatedly tried to help. She's the entire reason he got detention in the first place!*

The taller man sticks the key into the padlock, and I'm frozen, watching Jeffrey's smile widen as he reaches inside to grab Anna. The terror, rage and guilt all vie for dominance as I stare at my biological father. Each second that passes feels like a lifetime as his hand gets within an inch of her arm and I snap, surging forward to shove his shoulders hard.

He staggers back a step. "Why you—" His hand recoils across his chest before snapping it toward my cheek, and I dodge out of the way at the last second before the tall man grabs my hair in his fist. Next thing I know, my face collides against the shit covered floor before I'm being hoisted into the air by the tall man.

The other man with Jeffrey grabs Anna by the arm, and panic rises even faster as I throw my fists into the tall man's back, shrieking at him.

"Put me down!"

He ignores my hits, and they escort us out of the room as something hard slams against the side of my head.

I'm stunned. The room spins as stars speckle my vision, and it's not until my eyes find Jeffrey that I register the punch he landed.

"Shut the fuck up, dumb bitch." He spits with a look of pure disdain.

My head already hurt before this, and with the nausea rising in my stomach, I'm not sure how long I'll last without vomiting as they silently make their way out of the building into the night.

I debate screaming more, but the first punch was enough of a warning that I'm not the one in control here, and I still need to find out where Cole is.

My head feels light, and it gets hard to keep my eyes open. Every footfall shatters the silence, and I'm fading in and out of awareness as my blurred vision clears. Each second we gain distance from the buildings, I notice the familiar ruins as I squirm frantically.

*They're going to 'sanctify' us.*

*Shit.*

*I'm way too far over my fucking head.*

My movement does nothing to slow their pace as I hear the hidden door squeak open. The tall man carrying me takes heavy steps down into the hidden entrance, and the world as I know it grows farther away before the door closes, plunging us all into darkness.

Keeping my focus on Cole, finding him and escaping this place, it's all I can do to keep relatively calm as the haunting chant grows closer with each step.

*But why are they doing this? What the hell does this achieve?*

*What is the point?*

The chanting grows louder, and the tall man turns around, setting me down as my gaze lands on the masked men surrounding the circle with faces etched into deep frowns.

Blood stains the ground in the center of the circle, with stone pillars lining the room in five places that seem deliberately placed. Each man stands next to a pillar before one turns to face us.

"Bring the girl."

My heart drops, and the tall man spins me around to see Anna being dragged to the front.

"No." I whisper, feeling his grip on me tighten, and they shove Anna to her knees as the five masked men take places around her. "No!"

The tall man's hold on me is bruising, and I continue to squirm until the sharp edge of a blade presses against my throat. The bite of it forces me to straighten, and I watch in horror as Anna looks at the man in the center eagerly.

"Behold, the beauty of His blessings." Jeffrey whispers, as if what I'm about to witness will be the second coming of Jesus Christ himself.

All I can do is watch as Jeffrey moves to step in front of Anna, and tears stream down my cheeks as the men chant more animatedly. When their chant comes to a head, he raises his blade in the air, and in one swift movement brings it back down, burying it deep into her chest as she screams.

The sound is immediately cut off by gargling, and I watch with wide eyes as she drops to her knees like a stone. Her body twitches as the men continue to chant, letting her blood seep down her body and onto the surrounding floor.

*No.*

*Anna's dead.*

The men chant louder, and all I can do is watch in horror as the teenage girl falls forward in slow motion, and her body collapses in a heap as the chant comes to a crescendo.

Jeffrey is the first to stop, turning to look at me with blood splattered on his skin and a broad smile.

"Don't worry. It'll be your turn to join His army too. You're almost ready."

"What the hell are you talking about?"

He just grins, ignoring the vitriol in my voice as I struggle against the tall man's grip.

"You bastard! Where is my brother?! You'll pay for this!"

My mind is in a frenzy, and I thrash wildly as Jeffrey jerks his head to the side, the shit-eating grin still plastered across his face. "Put her in solitary until tomorrow night."

Tall man grunts in response before dragging me off to the side and I panic with each step we take in a new direction. The tall man cuts to the right behind the pillar to a narrow tunnel opening, and I'm scanning the endless darkness before we come out the other side. It's not long before he shoves me roughly into a cell and slams it shut behind me.

Enclosed on all sides with only a small opening near the bottom for what I can only assume is air, I already feel claustrophobic as the door rattles shut.

*Breathe, Az.*

The air feels thin, and I desperately gulp down breaths as half of me fights against the other.

*You're alive, just breathe.*

Another echo of a door sounds out, and my lungs catch in my chest, listening to the pairs of footsteps that disappear into the distance.

"Hello?" My voice sounds so small in the confines of this prison, and I hear a thud not far away. "Anyone there?"

Another thud sounds out, followed by a pained groan, and my eyes widen.

"Cole?"

Another thud, followed by another, fills the air before the faint sound of a deep breath.

"Az–" Cole's voice is muffled, and it sounds like he's mumbling into a pillow, but when the familiar three knocks sound out in the rhythm only we would know, relief washes over me.

Tears spring to my eyes as I shift closer to the door. "Cole, are you okay?"

Another pained moan sounds out, and my breath hitches as my tears fall in earnest.

*He's alive.*

*Thank fucking God.*

# Chapter 36

It's been hours since I heard Cole say my name.

Even though he hasn't spoken since, I've still heard moments of his breathing or snoring, and the occasional groan which tells me he's still alive at the very least.

For the first bit, I relished in the knowledge that he's okay, but after that was done, I started to look for a way out.

The issue is that there is none.

At least not from this room.

There's no way to open the door from the inside, the lock that I can see, and there are no weaknesses in any of the walls. No screws inside, no loose edges, or any way to force my way out.

After a few hours of searching, I'd fallen asleep from pure exhaustion with my head resting against the cold metal wall. Somewhere nearby, a constant drip of water fills the air, and I hang onto the sound, if only to keep my mind from spiraling.

A thud sounds out in the distance, followed by another.

Another two thuds follow, and my heart rattles in my chest as the next pair sounds closer than before.

*Footsteps.*

I jolt upright, scurrying to the back of the small cell with wide eyes straining against the invasive darkness. A metallic clanging fills the air and I listen with bated breath as a loud creak sounds out, followed by Cole's pained moans. The shuffling of footsteps passes by the front of my cell, and my heart rages in my chest.

*Is he being released?*

*How long have we even been in here?*

*Why is he still unable to speak? How badly did they hurt him?*

The padlock on my door rustles, and the door swings open, revealing Jeffrey on the other side as the pit in my stomach grows. "Times up, dumb bitch."

He leans inside, and with a bruising grip, hauls me out by my arm as I cry out, which only makes him more rough as we make our way out of the connecting tunnel to the main room.

Seeing the silhouette of the tall man hauling Cole alongside him keeps me in pace with Jeffrey until the desperation to get to him coats every inch of my being.

It looks like Cole can hardly walk by himself with how he's being towed along, and a fresh wave of concern hangs heavy on me. Tall man turns the corner up ahead, bringing them out of my line of sight as my steps quicken.

"Eager to walk to your end, huh?"

I nearly trip over my own feet as my eyes widen.

*He can't mean...*

*They wouldn't...*

My eyes lock with his beady gaze and the answering smirk he gives sends a fresh wave of panic down my spine.

*No.*

*Please, God, no.*

*I will take my end, but not Cole.*

*Not my baby brother.*

Turning to clasp my hand on top of his around my biceps, my voice is a hushed, urgent whisper. "Just take me." His grip tightens and amusement paints his features. "Only me. Please."

He pauses, reaching over to place his hand on mine as his features suddenly turn contemplative, and his brows furrow as he nods his head slightly. "Okay."

Surprise and relief wash over me as I search his face. "Wait, really?"

I glance to the end of the connecting tunnel mere feet away before shifting my gaze back to Jeffrey. Before I can lay my eyes on him, my head snaps to the side and pain blooms across my still swollen cheek.

"No, you dumb bitch. You're both being sanctified tonight in His name. You should be grateful that your worthless lives will be reborn in His image, even though you are unworthy of it."

My jaw gapes as a metallic taste fills my mouth.

*What the hell is he on about?*

Jeffrey moves again, tugging me along roughly to the edge of the room where they've already positioned Cole in the center. I watch them surround him, and when one masked man steps aside, he finally comes into view and my desperation bleeds into rage.

His face is varying shades of purple, swollen with gashes in his skin that look like they've reopened recently. His nose looks broken, and the bruising seems to continue beyond his clothes as I spot deep colored welts through the holes in his tattered shirt.

I surge forward in an instant to get to him, but I'm yanked back by my hair, and I stumble just as Jeffrey's large hand encircles my throat. He drags me backward, and I have to grip his arm to hold myself upright as he slams me against the stone wall.

The pressure of his palm is so brutal that I can hardly cry out at the pain, but the sound seems to snap Cole out of his stupor as his eyes lazily land on me.

My vision blurs from the tears pouring from my eyes, my only outlet for the desperation and rage in my body with nowhere to go, and I thrash, kicking at Jeffrey with all the strength in my body.

*No, if they're going to fucking kill us, I won't make it easy.*

One of my kicks lands on Jeffrey's knee, and he grunts, leaning awkwardly as I rake my nails against his face. He recoils ever so slightly, just enough for me to slip his grasp, and I make a break for Cole.

I only get two feet before someone yanks my hair again, sending me sprawling onto my backside with a thud. Pain shoots from my tailbone to my scalp, where I'm almost sure they ripped out some hair.

I'd be shocked if not.

"It's always the stupid ones that are the hardest to get under control." Jeffrey turns me to my stomach and, with my face roughly shoved into the hard floor. My arms are pulled behind my back, and I feel some kind of rope tightened around them as my heart sinks.

He uses the bindings to lift me to my feet, sending more pain through my body before he slams me into the wall with more force than necessary, as if making his point that he's in control once again.

"Now watch while your precious little brother gains a purpose for once in his fucking life."

My eyes find Cole, only to see tear streaks in the bloodstains on his face as he stares back at me, and my body shudders.

*I can't stop this.*

*We're both going to die here.*

The men in front of the pillars chant, and I hold Cole's gaze as my entire body trembles.

*I've failed him. As a sister, and as a friend.*

My tears fall to my chest, sending a bitter chill down my spine as shadows dance along the candlelight surrounding Cole.

I never should have let him go on the field trip. We should have just left the moment mom died, and we should have run away together.

The acrid taste of regret burns on my tongue as I consider what we could have done–should have done–differently.

But it's too late now.

Jeffrey turns to me with a sneer, and his hand moves to squeeze my throat as another man steps out from the shadows on the other side of the pillars, still obscured from the sight of the men encircling Cole.

"Say your prayers for him now, dumb bitch."

The chanting gets louder and echoes off the walls. My gaze slides from Cole to Jeffrey, but it's when the candles illuminate the tall figure standing behind Jeffrey that I realize God won't save us.

But the grey-eyed prince of hell wearing his black, form-fitting, well-tailored suit, and an expression of rage that mirrors my own, is the one coming to our rescue instead.

It's only then that my lips pull into a ghost of a smile.

Because I know that, despite the horror I felt at seeing Vassago's abilities and rage, he never directed them toward me.

No. He directed his aggression toward the two people who had simply hurt me and used their power in their favor.

"Perhaps it's your turn to pray, asshole."

Jeffrey frowns at my words, but his confusion lasts a mere moment before the chanting stops altogether. He turns to look at the masked men surrounding Cole as they all stagger back, looking themselves over with a sense of urgency.

Though I can't see his face in its entirety, I know the moment Jeffrey notices Vassago, because he stumbles, and Vassago takes another confident step out of the shadows.

"Tell me, false prophet, what will your God do to save you, I wonder?" Vassago's tongue clicks as he eyes Jeffrey, and the men surrounding Cole back away.

Sudden movement catches my eye as one masked man tries to run, but before he gets to the tunnel, his body crumples without so much of a sound beyond the thud of him hitting the cold, unforgiving floor.

"Please, stop." One man begs before another cries out, the blisters forming along his visible skin as another whimpers and drops to his knees.

Vassago glances between them coldly and blinks. "No."

Jeffrey's chest heaves to my right, seemingly unharmed as his lip curls into a snarl. "It's too late, anyway. You may have stopped us from getting these two, but we are only a small operation. You can't kill us all, demon."

Vassago's eyes flick to mine as Jeffrey emphasizes the last word, like he's looking for any sign of my surprise or to gauge my reaction.

But he won't find one.

No, in the time I've been away from him, I've come to my own conclusions about who and what he is.

Jeffrey whirls on me. "And you! He has turned you against your own kind, dumb bitch. He's turned you into a whore for filth! You don't know who this bastard really is!"

I ignore Jeffrey's screams, because even if I don't know everything, I know enough.

He is Vassago, a renown attorney, a prince of hell, and a demon with abilities that would make every man, woman, and child run for the hills.

*But I will not.*

"Enough of this." Jeffrey steps to my left, and he yanks me to his side as Vassago takes a quick step to follow us. I'm shoved to the ground as Jeffrey shrieks in pain, but his cries quickly quiet down, turning into raucous laughter as I roll to my side.

Vassago glances around at the ground with his brows pulled together in tense concern before he looks up, and I see the odd symbols marked in a circle on the ceiling, like something you'd see in a movie where they summon a demon, but he can't leave the perimeter.

Jeffrey turns to me with a triumphant smile. "See! Now you are free from the demon's influence. Look within and know that you have been saved!"

Blinking, I glance between him and Vassago as Jeffrey's words sink in.

I watch Vassago, trapped and unable to use his power on Jeffrey, glaring at him as if he wishes with everything in his being that he could step out from this invisible cage.

It's not until his gaze turns to me that my thoughts suddenly spiral. *Was I really being influenced? Manipulated by his power?*

A long moment passes, and Jeffrey's eager face fills my vision. "Tell me you feel different." His words are demanding, and I suck in a ragged breath.

It took me a few seconds of contemplation, self assessment and a fresh perspective to really see everything clearly for once in my life.

"I am free from his manipulation."

Jeffrey's face contorts into pure elation; I shift my gaze to the stone-faced Vassago as Jeffrey turns away.

But I wasn't finished.

Vassago's guarded expression makes my gut wrench, and when his eyes meet mine, I hold them, forcing my voice out louder than before. "I have **always** been free from it."

He jerks to look at me just as I thrust my feet into the back of his knees, and he buckles forward. Vassago reacts quickly as Jeffrey crosses the threshold of the circle, grasping him by the collar of his shirt.

Dragging him to the center of the circle, Vassago shoves him to the ground before half-kneeling on his body. The fury on Vassago's face is palpable, and within seconds Jeffrey starts to panic. His legs kick, and he claws at Vassago's arms before his shrieks fill the air.

It takes a few long moments before I understand what's happening, and Vassago leans over him with a glare I wouldn't wish upon my worst enemy. The light colored groin of Jeffrey's jeans darken as his voice gives out, and I almost think he's soiled himself when a pop fills the air. Blood seeps through the material as my eyes widen.

*Did he just–? Did his balls just—?*

Vassago's whispers carry in the still air of the room, and the vicious promise sends a chill down my spine. "Mark my words. This is going to hurt, but regretfully nowhere near enough."

My mind registers what he says just as he grasps Jeffrey's body and hurls him into the air. Everything is in slow motion as a scream tears from Jeffrey's throat, and within a heartbeat, his body crashes into the ceiling with a thunderous crack. The stone ceiling shudders from the impact, and his body comes crashing down as a long, deep fracture splits the symbols, and three more long lines web outward from it.

Shallow, gasping breaths come from Jeffrey before he exhales for the last time, and the adrenaline of the entire ordeal finally dissipates from my veins as Cole crawls over, wincing with each movement.

*It's over. We survived.*

Vassago stands to his full height, stepping out of the now fractured circle to kneel at my side, gently tugging on my bindings before they go slack, and he unwinds it all from my arms.

When he's done, I feel his hand move to support my back as he helps me sit up, and in that same moment, Cole collapses into my chest, wrapping his arms around my torso. When I encircle my arms around him, he sobs.

My gaze meets Vassago's, seeing his features relaxed, and if I didn't know any better, I'd say he's relieved. "How did you find us?"

He grins and shrugs nonchalantly. "My brother and I have a knack for finding things, and people."

I have so many questions I want to ask him, but I push them down, focusing on the present as much as we can.

And although I'm not always known for my patience, for these answers, I can wait.

After a long moment, Vassago pushes to his feet, and I gently pat Cole's back. "Come on, kiddo. Let's get out of here."

By the time we're all upright, the battered state we're in is abundantly clear, and with Vassago's help, we hobble through the tunnel toward the hidden entrance as my mind wanders to the cages in the buildings.

"What about the others?"

Vassago's hand remains ever so gently at the small of my back as he remains focused on the path. "Seir and Oriana are outside with the FBI helping reunite the children with their families."

A wave of relief washes over me, but I can't help but wonder how many families will have lost their children to these assholes.

I freeze, knowing that I need to rip the band-aid off as Vassago pauses beside me. It's not until Cole realizes we've stopped, and he turns to look at me that I feel something inside of me shatter.

"What?"

My heart feels like it's breaking as I prepare to give my little brother another blow, but this one won't be physical.

"Last night... they..." I choke down a sob, and I see Vassago's jaw tense in my peripherals. "They 'sanctified' Anna... I tried to stop it but there were too many of them, and they—"

Tears pour down his cheeks, and his head tilts up as his shoulders shake.

I've seen Cole cry throughout most of my life, but this time, it just feels different. It doesn't take much for me to realize that Anna was more than just someone he stuck up for at school.

"I'm so sorry, Cole."

He shakes his head, but says nothing before heading down the tunnel once more, and Vassago's thumb glides along my back soothingly before I follow close behind him.

There's a long moment of silence as we near the hidden door, and Cole's trembling voice carries in the air. "I convinced her to come with me."

My heart drops again, and I feel a fresh wave of bitter anger toward the dead men who already paid the price.

"She didn't want to go, but I told her Father Arrenault's camp could be a way to spend time together, and I could teach her the prayers so she wouldn't get expelled. It's my fault she's dead."

Vassago steps past us to the door, but pauses, and turns to face Cole with a contemplative look. "I'm no counselor, and I'm hardly the person to be giving life advice, but from where I stand, she made the choice on her own whether to attend. And if she chose to spend the time with you, then do not tarnish her memory with self blame, for surely she would want better for you than to wallow in self-pity."

My gaze flicks to Cole, and I watch him absorb Vassago's words, staring at the prince of hell as a rogue tear trails down his cheek.

Cole nods and exhales a ragged breath. "At least all these assholes are dead."

Vassago opens the hidden door and shakes his head. "Not all of them."

# Chapter 37

Cole's hand slips into mine, and Vassago pushes the hidden door open as blue and red flashing lights illuminate the treeline in the dark.

"If you'd still wish for me to represent you, and well, even if not, I'd advise you not to answer unnecessary questions. If they request a statement, keep it short and to the facts." He glances between us. "That goes for either of you."

My chest tightens, and I nod. "Your trusted counsel hasn't driven us astray thus far, Vassago."

The flicker of concern behind his eyes seems to melt away as he inclines his head before stopping us. "They will offer you an ambulance and medical care. I need you to trust me and decline it."

I frown, glancing at Cole. His swollen, bruised eye, and gashes in his face have me worried, but when I look at the determination and certainty in Vassago's features, I just nod.

"Right. No medical care. Got it."

Footsteps approach from the nearest building and I turn to see Seir and Oriana, their expressions hesitant as they glance between us. But it's Oriana who speaks first as she steps in close. "A stupid question, but a necessary one. Are you both alright?"

I huff a dry laugh and nod as pain radiates in my head. "All things considered, I think we're fine."

She nods. "Good. We've contacted a handful of families so far and cleared out the cages, but the FBI is going to be here a while."

As if summoned, more footsteps filled the air, and two officers approached from behind, flashing their badges at me and Cole. The closer officer, a younger brunette woman, adjusts her cap.

"I'm special agent Rodelle. This is my partner, special agent Thorne. May I ask your names?"

I glance at Vassago, who inclines his head, before my attention turns to the agents in front of us. "I'm Azura Leclair, and this is my little brother, Cole Leclair."

Agent Thorne jots down our names on a notepad as Rodelle glances behind Vassago. "Where did you all come from?"

Vassago's eyes are encouraging, and I suck in a breath. "There's a hidden passage there." I point to the exposed floorboards. "They had us held there for the past day or so."

Rodelle's eyes widen, and she glances at Thorne before pulling her radio out and murmuring into it. "Is there anyone else down there?"

I shake my head. "I don't know. There are tunnels, so there could be."

"Christ." Thorne breathes, jotting something else down as Rodelle blinks.

"How did you two escape?"

My heart thunders. "They were preoccupied, or something. I think they forgot about us or didn't think we were in any state to get away. By the time we got out, there were bodies lying around, and we just ran."

Rodelle goes to ask another question, and Vassago steps forward. "I believe that's enough for today, Special Agent Rodelle. My clients have been through much, as I'm sure you can see."

She glances between us and must realize the state we're in as she nods. "Right, I'll call the paramedics over—"

"No need." She halts and looks between us with her brows furrowed. "We just need a bath, some ice, and a good night's sleep. We'll be okay."

She still doesn't look convinced, but she inclines her head, respectively. "Remain on scene, but you can go to your attorney's vehicle, Mr. and Ms. Leclair. We may still need a written statement."

I nod, exhaling a ragged breath before Seir, Oriana and Vassago lead the way to their cars. Each step brings us closer to the newly freed kids, and my heart aches at how distant they all seem.

There's a familiarity in the absence of tears in their eyes, and the disassociating hits too close to home. Too many times, I went through a traumatic event and sought refuge away from my mind. It becomes a prison of its own after a while because you can't afford to break when stakes are high.

Staying quiet, I slide into the back seat of Vassago's car and Cole climbs in alongside me. Vassago peers into the back, searching my face for a long moment like he has something to say, but his attention catches on the FBI agents approaching, and he shuts the door.

The front door opens, and Oriana climbs into the front seat before shutting the door and locking it. There's a long moment of silence until Cole shifts in his seat, and seconds later he's eased his head into my lap.

I watch Oriana's gaze scan over the crowd of children before she watches Seir talk to an agent.

"You don't seem surprised by any of this."

She turns her head to look over her shoulder at me, and her gaze drops to Cole before she murmurs. "When I met Seir, it was because I was going through one of the hardest times in my life, and I was the target of something I was oblivious to." She gestures to the children and buildings as my stomach twists.

Cole's breathing evens out, and he snores as my fingers run over his crusted hair.

"When I learned who Seir really was, I ran away, and my best friend became their target in my absence. My biggest mistake was running away because I was too afraid to face what I'd been taught to fear."

My throat constricts, and I shake my head in disbelief. "Her death was why you said there were demons in this world. You were talking about them."

She nods. "I miss her every day, but she didn't just disappear. She lives on elsewhere, and I know that she's probably kicking someone's ass wherever her soul went after the ritual."

I frown. "What do you mean?"

She blinks and chews her lip as if wondering where to start. "The ritual sends the soul to be in their God's army. They create environments of trauma, tragedy, fear, or famine to turn people to God, then complete the rituals to add the newly departed souls to their army after death. When I met Seir, they were teaching my entire class how to complete these rituals under the guise of theology studies."

*This was happening in her town. Could it really be this far spread?*

My mind wanders to Blackwell's flagrant dismissal of the school's malpractice, and my entire body runs cold. He was so happy when mom passed, but that was the day of the funeral and Cole's field trip.

*He's either involved or complacent...*

My eyes widen as I stare at her and my heart feels like it's beating a mile per minute as someone waves in front of the windshield, catching her attention.

"Shoot, I need to go see what they need. Just stay here, okay? I'll lock the doors." She hurries out, and the doors click as the locks engage before she jogs over to the group of children standing next to one of the FBI agents.

"Do you think she was telling the truth?"

Hearing his muffled words, I glance down at Cole's still battered face and nod.

"She has no reason to lie about any of that, and after what we saw back there, it sounds like what they were trying to do."

Another long moment passes before his sleepy voice fills the air once more. "So Anna isn't dead?"

"By the sounds of it, she's been enlisted into an army."

He shifts to be more comfortable, and I continue to run my fingers through his tangled hair.

"Thank you for coming after me, Az."

My chest squeezes, and I squeeze my eyes shut, fighting back tears. "I made a promise. I intended to keep it."

# Chapter 38

By the time the FBI agents finally let us leave, we're pulling onto the path toward the main road and exhaustion has my eyes fighting to stay open.

The car shifts back and forth methodically along the uneven road, and the panicked parking job I'd done on my way here comes to the forefront of my mind as I groan.

Oriana looks over her shoulder as Seir peers in the rearview. "What's wrong?"

"My car. I left it at the entrance to the maintenance driveway."

Seir points off to the right as we break through the treeline to the main road. "This way?"

I nod, and Oriana blows out a tense breath. "I can drive Vassago's car and follow you home."

Seir looks at her with wide eyes. "Are you sure?"

She just nods, and even though she's smiling, I can tell she's uncomfortable as guilt rifles through me.

We pull off the shoulder of the road near the maintenance entrance, and bright headlights illuminate where we're parked as Vassago's engine shuts off.

Seir and Oriana get out of the car, and I glance at Cole's limp form, fast asleep against the opposite door before getting out myself.

"Is everything alright?" Vassago's brows pinch together as Oriana walks over to him, murmuring something before understanding flashes across his face.

He nods, and his attention flicks to me as he moves from the door to let Oriana climb in. His engine rumbles to life, and she pulls up beside Seir, rolling the passenger window down as Vassago steps up to my side.

"Race you home?" I can hear the smile in Seir's teasing voice as Ori huffs a laugh.

"Not a chance. You're a maniac."

Vassago moves to my side and waves to Seir as they pull off the shoulder and onto the main road. Their tail lights get further away, and Vassago turns to face the maintenance path.

His expression pulls into a grimace, and he glances at me. "What in the world was this parking job, Az?"

I follow his gaze to see a long scratch from a branch and the vehicle is angled awkwardly in the path as I wince.

"I might not have been in my right mind."

His brow raises, and his grey eyes narrow on me. "Pray, do tell."

Chewing the inside of my cheek, I climb into the passenger's seat. "I took mom's sleeping pills, but they didn't help me sleep... and I might have left to find Cole while I was still out of it."

His eyebrows shoot up, and he shakes his head. "Never, ever again."

My hand raises into the air, and I bring the other over my heart solemnly. "Scout's honor."

He turns the ignition and pulls out of the awkward position as I chew the inside of my cheek nervously. My curiosity has become insatiable now, and with no one else around, I can't help myself.

"How did you find us, Vassago?"

His features turn contemplative, but he glances at me and sighs. "The answer to that question depends on how much you want to know."

I frown. "Everything."

A genuine huff of laughter escapes him as he smirks. "Right. Well, you have seen the blisters and boils... and are still here." He backs up and tosses me a sidelong glance. "But what you don't know about me is, that much like my brother, we both can observe glimpses of the various paths the future may hold."

My mouth drops open, and suddenly, it all makes so much more sense. "So when you said the case had so many variations..."

He nods. The car rocks from side to side as we get onto the main road, and he shifts into drive. "It was because there were too many variables and paths at that point to see which way it was going to end."

Blowing out a breath, he glances over with a hint of exasperation on his face. "However, when it comes to you specifically, it appears you are a blind spot in that ability. I could peer into the future, but whenever I looked for yours, it came up blank. It would appear that this blind spot also applied to my ability to find things."

I know I said I wanted to know everything, and I do, but damn if this isn't information overload.

He purses his lips thoughtfully. "When you said Cole wasn't responding, I started looking for him, but naturally, these societies of people doing these God-forbidden rituals have gotten smarter recently. They've found a way to hide themselves from us, which delayed my ability to find you as quickly as I'd wanted. When you didn't respond to my text in the morning, something just felt... wrong. I ended up breaking into the school, finding where the location of Cole's camp was. Seir called his contact in the FBI, and we came straight here."

Reflecting on not responding to his messages, guilt rifles through me, and I wring my hands in my lap. "Vassago, I need to tell you something." His gaze slides to me, and I inhale a deep, steadying breath. "I saw what happened to the medic and the cop."

He stiffens in his seat, blinks, and his attention flicks between the road and me once more. "You saw—"

"All of it."

His jaw tenses, and his knuckles turn white as he grips the wheel. "So you were avoiding me because of that?"

I shake my head. "I wasn't ignoring you, I just—"

"You don't need to explain yourself, Az."

"I don't think it's fair to you if I don't."

He raises a brow, and a hint of humor paints his features. "You watched me murder two people, and somehow I'm the one who deserves an explanation?"

"I—" Pausing for a moment, my mouth opens and snaps shut as I consider it. "Well, we both deserve explanations, then."

He just laughs harder and shrugs. "I did tell you I was going to kill them."

I consider him for a moment and nod. "And I didn't ask you about it because I didn't know what to think about the fact that you killed them. I just convinced myself it had to be a mistake, or refused to acknowledge it because of everything happening with Cole, and the school... I had just learned that magic was real days before witnessing your ability to literally kill people."

There's a long moment of silence between us, and his grey eyes slide to mine. "Do you fear me, Azura?"

I hold his gaze for a heartbeat before he returns his attention to the road, and instead of responding immediately, I really consider his question.

I think back to the stream, and how I felt in that moment seeing him take two people's lives like it was nothing. It's already clear that my terror in that moment was not because of his abilities, but that I didn't know who he really was.

My fear was the unknown.

Each moment since then has led me to place my faith in him in more ways than one, and I shake my head.

"I do not fear you, Vassago."

Reaching over, I slide my hand into his palm, and his fingers intertwine with mine.

"Good. You've never needed to, nor will you ever." His lips twitch upward. "That said, Rennensberg High School? They, on the other hand, should fear me."

I huff a quiet laugh as we pull into Seir and Oriana's driveway. There's already three cars there, and one of them looks like a brand-new electric SUV.

"Whose car is that?"

Vassago just grins. "Our other brother, Stolas."

My stomach flips, and I nod, but Vassago just laughs harder.

"Relax, Az. He's fine. He works with all things medicinal, and we called him to come check you and your brother out."

I nod again as he puts the car into park, and we slowly make our way inside, hearing indistinct conversation from the kitchen.

We're walking around the corner as Seir and Oriana come into view at one end of the table, watching intently as a man stands in front of Cole.

His back is to us, so I don't get a good look at him until we take a few steps further into the kitchen, and he turns at the sound of our footsteps. His dark brunette hair is near black, but it's his eyes that suck me in first. They're bright and speckled sky blue with patches of verdant that make his iris look like their own worlds.

"You must be Cole's sister, Azura." His deep voice resonates in the room, and it's at this moment that I realize I'm standing in a room of not one, not two, but three princes of hell.

I nod, and he motions for me to come sit beside Cole.

Reluctantly letting go of Vassago's hand, I slide in next to Cole and wait as he reaches over into his bag and rifles through it. Shoving items into a smaller bag, he hands it to Cole.

"Boil this into a tea tonight before bed. Don't drive anything or lift anything heavy–" He glances at Vassago. "And don't sign anything important. It'll make you drowsy and that's normal, but tomorrow you'll feel right as rain, with minimal swelling. I do need to set your nose, though."

He stands and crowds Cole's space as the big sister in me fights the urge to get between them. His arms jerk as a snap sounds out, and Cole groans.

"That should do. One cup tonight is all you should need, the benefits will last up to five days."

He turns to me, and the moment his hand moves to my cheek, I pull backward instinctively. Stolas' head tilts as he assesses me for a long moment, and I feel like I'm under a microscope when he pulls a chair in front of me.

"Where is your pain, and what caused it?"

I glance at Vassago before answering. "The side and back of my head, my neck, my tailbone and my cheek. They punched me in the head a couple of times and threw me to the ground. My head hit the stone hard. They shoved me backward, I fell on my tailbone, and one of them backhanded me across the face."

"I knew I should have dragged out their deaths more." Vassago mutters and Oriana giggles.

"But at least they're dead." I muse before turning my gaze back to Stolas as he looks at me thoughtfully.

"Sagittarius?"

I blink at him and nod. "How'd you know?"

He just shrugs, and rifles through his bag some more. "Just a hunch. Here–" He holds out a small bag of herbs. "Same thing as your brother, just nowhere near as potent."

He pushes to his feet and steps over to clasp arms with Vassago.

"Not staying the night?"

Stolas turns to Oriana with a smile and shakes his head. "Afraid not. Things are bad back home."

Seir nods once before clasping his arm and pulling Stolas in for a hug. "Good to see you, brother."

When they break, Stolas' eyes flick to me once more, and he reaches into his bag, searching for a long moment before pulling out a golden bracelet with various shaped stones hanging from it.

"Here." He offers the bracelet between us, and I tentatively take it. "It should help you with regulating your energies, and centering your nervous system, particularly for physical connection to others."

I blink and glance back down at the bracelet. "I, uh, thank you."

He just nods, and Seir walks with him to the hallway. "Are you still firm in your decision?"

I see Stolas shake his head as they disappear around the corner and out of sight.

"So, that was your brother?" Cole asks, and Vassago nods his head.

"One of many." He grins, and Oriana walks over, offering her palm between us.

"I'll make your tea, if you both want to go shower." She scrunches her nose, as if to emphasize that we smell, and I can't help but laugh as I push to my feet.

"Yeah, yeah. I'll go get un-stinky." Cole grumbles the same, and we head to the two bathrooms to get cleaned up.

Truth be told, I've been able to smell my stench for the past hour and I can't wait to get clean.

# Chapter 39

I don't know how long it's been by the time I've gotten a change of clothes, a towel and gotten the shower turned to sweltering heat, but what I do know, is that I'm desperate to clean off. Even with the faucet turned the entire way, the cool water is still warming, and I peel off my crusted clothes that smell like blood, urine and shit.

It's a shock that Cole could even rest with his head in my lap earlier.

I suppose he was exhausted, though.

Glancing at my reflection in the mirror, I see the angry purple welt on the side of my face, and my skin is covered in mud and various other things that make me want to gag.

The urge to get clean is stronger than ever, and I climb into the lukewarm water, sighing contentedly as a soft knock sounds out.

I frown. "Who is it?"

Another moment goes by before the door slowly creaks open a sliver, and Vassago peers in.

"May I?"

My heart suddenly feels like it's a stampede in my chest, and I nod. "Yes."

He closes the door behind him, and I watch as he peels off his clothes. His back muscles flex as he pulls each off, tossing them aside before standing just outside the shower door, gesturing toward me with a silent question.

His tattoos on full display in the light like this, beautifully inked over a canvas of hard muscle, sends desire pooling in my core. I nod, feeling that unending pull to be close to him, and he opens the door with a click before stepping inside. The water pelts the top of my head as he gazes down at me with a soft expression.

Everything he said to me the day I met Seir and Oriana comes full front and center, and I watch as he wordlessly reaches over to grab the second shower head.

But I get it now, even if I still have questions.

"So," I whisper, and his piercing gaze settles on me. "Is it normal for two princes of hell to fall in love with humans?"

Vassago's eyes flash, and I know it's because I've already put together that Seir must also be a prince of hell, if only because of his name.

Not to mention that I saw Seir listed on one of the sites.

... And Stolas.

"No. It is not typical. Seir has spent years trying to understand why Oriana entered his life in the manner she did..." He tilts his head slightly, and massages water against a tender part of my scalp from where my hair was possibly ripped out. "I suspect we may never get an answer."

I frown. "Why not?"

A dry, bitter amusement dances across his features. "Because as with everything Father does, much of it is a riddle or a complicated puzzle with missing words or pieces. By the time you think you've found the answer, or seen the vision, you find another that throws you on another path."

*So... God really is real then.*

The knowledge sends a wave of anger through my veins. "Isn't that frustrating? Can't you just ask Him? Why isn't He stopping them?"

Vassago's features turn somber, and something tells me I won't get the entire truth out of him as he sighs. "It's complicated, Az.

We're here to help curb the influence they have, but they've grown bold, and there are rules. Rules that I broke tonight by intervening."

My eyes widen. "Rules?!"

He inclines his head. "We cannot directly change course through action. We can influence change, and whisper in people's ears, but taking lives, using human-made infrastructure for inhuman reasons... it is strictly forbidden and punishable by death. True death."

I swallow hard at the thought that the wrong move could have meant his end, and he brings the shower head around to rinse off my body.

"Since Azrael himself hasn't slain Seir and me where we stand, it seems these rules are changing. Without direct communication with Father or Samael, we're flying blind on exactly how that might be. Seir, Oro, and I have been doing our best to use our abilities, but it's still not enough. We are not unified in our efforts, and while we have been gaining ground, it's not happening fast enough. I fear that while we might win the minor battles, we cannot simply end all their lives. We are losing this war."

*Samael. God. War.*

"Holy shit." I breathe. "Unholy, actually." I correct myself, and he laughs quietly under his breath.

His movements are slow, deliberate and filled with words he's not said as he works his fingers through the lengths of my hair once more. I trace the lines of his tattoos as he carefully massages the water through my locks.

To think this man could end my life in an instant without using his hands, the same man who has killed for me, who has hurt people, and protected not just me but Cole... is the same man—or demon, rather— who's taking such gentle care of me.

My chest squeezes to the point of pain.

When he's satisfied with rinsing me off, and the water's deliciously warm, he squeezes some shampoo into his hand. His fingers work through my hair, massaging from my scalp through the lengths before rinsing and repeating. The moment he brushes a tender area, I wince, and he eases pressure to a featherlight touch. He remains completely silent as he does the same with the conditioner, before gently scrubbing body wash over every inch of my body.

"Can I confess something?" He whispers as I squeeze a small amount of shampoo into my palm. My gaze flicks to his before I reach up to work it into his hair, and his eyes flutter as they threaten to roll back.

"I'm not a priestess, but you can confess what you'd like."

His eyes snap open with heat and warning, but he turns serious once more as I continue to massage the shampoo into his scalp.

"I know you likely felt uncomfortable when I killed those men, Az," his throat bobs. "But my confession is that I would have killed many, many more, if it meant keeping you from leaving this world." I reach over to grasp the removable shower head to rinse the shampoo from his hair. "Does that change your mind about me?"

I'm quiet for a moment as I consider his statement, but end up shaking my head.

"It does not change my mind at all." Reaching over to massage the conditioner into his hair, I reach for the body wash next and pause. "Someone once told me that the right thing to do is not always inherently good."

He gets a twinkle in his eye as his lips twitch. "That person must have been very smart."

The genuine laugh that escapes me has Vassago staring at me with a ghost of a smile that I never want to see fade.

# Chapter 40

A loud vibration fills the air as I groan, reaching for my cell on the wooden bedside table.

When I reach it, hearing the sound continue and my phone isn't the one vibrating, I roll over into Vassago's arms.

"That's you." I whisper, feeling his arms encircle my shoulders, tucking me closer into his chest. He exhales into my hair, and I don't know if my heart could swell more without exploding.

"They'll leave a message if it's urgent."

The sound stops, and for a heartbeat, I think it's done until it vibrates once more. He sighs, and when he reaches over to grab his cell, I notice the unknown caller ID as he swipes to answer.

"Gloam legal, how can I–"

A voice carries from the speaker, but it's so low as he holds the phone to his ear that I can't make out what they're saying.

"Interesting. When?" His thumb glides along my shoulder as he listens, and I feel him press his lips to my hair. "I'll discuss with Ms. Leclair and reach out with an answer by the end of the day. Thank you."

The line clicks, and he slides his phone to the side table before pulling me more into his chest.

A long moment passes, and my curiosity is eating at me when my mouth drops open to ask, but he just chuckles knowingly.f

"That," he whispers, "was the journalist for Channel Five News wanting to interview you. They also said that they have some information that we might be interested in hearing."

My heart stutters, and I push onto my elbow to look at him. "You're joking."

He laughs under his breath, and the way he smiles makes my throat clog with emotion. I feel his fingertips trail up my arm and shiver.

"I'd never joke about something so serious." He tucks a lock of my hair behind my ear, and moves my bangs from my eyes. "Do you feel up to speaking with them today, or another time?"

I know what he's really asking me, and that's if I'm okay to relive the experience all over again, because that's exactly what is going to happen as I explain everything.

Still, as much as I don't want to reopen the wound so soon, it's best to reopen it while it's fresh.

"We can do it today." His eyes widen, and his mouth drops open, but I shake my head. "I'm certain."

He nods and hesitates, which has me on high alert as my eyes narrow on him.

"What is it?" Anxiety builds in me when he doesn't answer, and I gently rest my hand on his chest. "Vassago, please tell me."

I can tell from the look on his face that he's choosing his words carefully. "Following the incident at Father Arrenault's camp, the FBI found the entire Rennensberg board of directors dead in the tunnels."

I gape at him. "The entire board?"

He nods, his grey eyes still searching my face, and I can already tell there's more. "The FBI have also arrested Father Arrenault, along with Mr. Green and Mr. Humphrey for human trafficking, human enslavement, kidnapping, and murder."

My entire body goes numb, and I blow out a breath as Vassago rubs gentle circles along the back of my hands.

"They were in on it the whole time?"

Vassago searches my face before he nods. "I'm afraid so."

A long moment passes and I let out a dry laugh. "I guess that explains why Cole was being targeted so much. At least all those kids are getting justice."

Vassago nods sadly. "And our dear Oriana, too."

I frown at him. "Why Ori?"

"The story is hers to tell, but suffice to say, she was also a victim of Arrenault's malpractice."

I blow out a breath. "There's so many people that have been affected or had their lives changed by these zealots. I don't understand how they thought that what they were doing was right."

Vassago eyes me for a moment, before tucking a lock of hair behind my ear, and I revel in the contact.

"What is right is not always good. What is good for one may be at the cost of another. It's a matter of perception."

I let his words sink in, and file through the life-changing information he's shared within the past five minutes.

His gaze drops to my mouth, and my body warms. "Well, we better start getting ready soon, so we're not late for the interview." In contrast to his words, he leans forward and his hand curls around the back of my neck as his lips press to mine.

Soon.

# Chapter 41

"Ms. Leclair, it's wonderful to meet you." Casey Warner smiles warmly from the chair next to me.

My heart's been racing since we left the house, and I feel like my answering smile is more of a grimace. "Nice to meet you as well, Casey."

Technically, we'd met in the back dressing rooms informally, because the makeup artist wanted to cover my bruises, and I'd refused, which apparently caused more of a scene than they wanted.

Because of my injuries, they had to play a content warning prior to the show airing, which apparently cost them more money than I could imagine.

Whatever that means.

"So, I know we have limited time together. Are you sure you're alright if we ask you a few questions about recent events?"

My palms grow clammy, and I nod. "Of course."

Casey's expression is somber as a man behind the cameras signals to Casey, and he glances down at his paperwork. "As we have been covering this week, Rennensberg High School had all of its board members found dead in an underground tunnel system after the FBI raided the campsite property of a member of the local church, Father Arrenault. Here with me is Azura Leclair, one survivor of said campsite. It's my understanding that you were there at the time of this raid. Is that correct?"

I nod. "Yes, that is correct."

"Now, understandably, the investigation is still ongoing, but clearly, we can see evidence of some things that occurred there."

I nod again. "Worse. Worse things happened, Casey."

He searches my face for a long moment and nods. "What can you tell us about Father Arrenault?"

"He was known by Rennensberg High School as an active partner between them and Divine Covenant. He had multiple after-school programs, but what he was most well known for was his religious rehabilitation facility. I only discovered recently that these facilities shared space with the campsite Rennensberg High school used for field trips."

Casey nods as he listens before glancing down at his paper. "So you said he partnered with Divine Covenant. Now, Channel Five News has recently uncovered that Divine Covenant has been lobbying politicians to pass legislation such as the HB-4952-34 which up front was a budgeting bill, but tagged onto it was a clause that would give churches and religious facilities less federal and state oversight. Essentially this would allow these organizations to function autonomously, and self govern. An example is the recent supreme court hearing on Henry vs. Lovette, where Divine Covenant was observed to have donated 10.9 million dollars to the companies owned by the spouses of the court. The courts haven't decided this case yet, but we predict a ruling in Henry's favor. This decision, as we know, would strip away the rights of those who place themselves willingly into the hands of any religious organization. It would also allow public schools to force students to learn one religion only instead of having a variety like we do today."

My breathing picks up, and I'm feeling grossly out of my element as Casey glances at his paper once more.

"Now, we also recently discovered that there was yet another player in this game, submitted by an anonymous tip that our researchers have since validated. So, Ms. Leclair, why don't you tell us how you came about this case against Rennensberg High School."

"Right, yeah. So, I was working for Blackwell Law Firm at the time and I received a call from my brother that he'd gotten detention. Originally, you know, I assumed he was just being a kid, but I later found out it was because they were holding mandatory prayer and gave him detention for not participating."

Casey's eyebrows shoot up. "And was this a private school?"

I shake my head, feeling tears form in the corners of my eyes at the part I will need to get out. "No. This was a public, state funded school." His jaw goes slack, but he lets me continue. "So I thought perhaps it was a mistake or something. Turns out the school had a 'three strikes, you're out' policy for missing mandatory prayer, and my little brother was just trying to–"

My breath hitches as the image of Anna comes to mind, and I squeeze my eyes shut. Tears trail down my cheeks, and I swipe at them.

The couch dips, and a hand slides into mine as my eyes flutter open to where Vassago now sits beside me. His eyes are encouraging, and I take a ragged breath.

"My little brother was trying to help his classmate Anna, who didn't know the prayers. He didn't want her to be expelled."

Tears pour down my face as Casey tosses me an apologetic look. He reaches over to a piece of paper lying face down and picks it up, holding it to face the camera. "This is young Annabell Kenneth. Anna was in her first year of high school, and they found her body in the tunnels under Arrenault's property. I know it is an active investigation, but Ms. Leclair, do you know what happened to young Anna?"

My hand squeezes Vassago's and I nod as my breath catches in my throat. "I do." The image of her being run through forces its way into my mind and I blow out a breath.

*Fuck, this is so much harder than I thought.*

Casey places the image down and out of sight, but I don't miss the tears in the corner of his eyes as he passes a box of tissues over.

"I know this has to be so hard for you, Ms. Leclair, so thank you again for being willing to meet with us on such short notice. I know our time is coming to an end, but we have one more question for you."

I nod, and Vassago's thumb gliding over the back of my hand keeps me grounded as I brace for the last question that Vassago urged me to ensure I answer.

"When you brought the case to Rennensberg High School, you went with Gloam Legal instead of Blackwell Law Firm. Why is that?"

The air catches in my lungs, and I glance at Vassago before returning my attention to the journalist. "Because Blackwell Law Firm was the only law firm in the city, and when I brought him the case initially, he stated there was nothing there. He told me he would expect my resignation on his desk the day that I serve papers to Rennensberg High School."

Casey nods. "And did you? Resign, I mean."

I shake my head. "No. The day after Rennensberg High School was served, Blackwell Law Firm was hired to represent them, and because of a conflict of interest, I was placed on an indefinite administrative leave."

Vassago squeezes my hand twice in reassurance, and I nearly sag with relief. Whatever future he sees with my answer must be good.

Casey glances down once more before his attention turns to me. "Fascinating. We here at Channel Five News did some digging into Blackwell Law Firm, and we actually found some interesting stuff. For example," He turns to the camera, addressing the audience directly. "Blackwell Law Firm has been in business for over fifty years, with thirty-five being under the Blackwell name. However, of those fifty years, we found one large annual donation per year to the firm from none other than Divine Covenant."

My eyes widen, and everything clicks into place. When I glance over at Vassago, he's already got a knowing look in his expression, and I'm in a state of shock as Casey continues.

"Furthermore, it appears as though there is some connection with Divine Covenant helping Blackwell Law Firm monopolize the city based on some strategic investments made by the organization around the same time when each competitor landed in the city."

My heart pounds. *No way. Blackwell was in league with Divine Covenant?*

I glance over at Vassago, and he squeezes my hand as his gaze meets mine.

*He knew this entire time. He knew, but couldn't do anything about it.*

Casey turns toward me. "I'd like to thank you for your time, Ms. Leclair. I hope you, your brother and the rest of the victims of this atrocity find justice." He looks at the camera once more. "When we come back, we'll cover the unrest overseas, as many question our support of the war that people are claiming has become a one-sided massacre. I'm Casey Warner, and this is Channel Five News."

"... Two minutes!" someone shouts from the back, and Casey turns to Vassago and me.

"You were brilliant. Thank you for coming."

I just nod, and Vassago reaches over to shake his hand as we all push to our feet. We're following an admin to the main exit when Vassago's phone rings.

He pauses by the doors to answer, and his eyes meet mine. "Is that right? And is that correspondence currently waiting in my email?"

The way he's looking at me makes it impossible not to eavesdrop, and a smile starts to creep across his face as he huffs a laugh. "I'll talk to Azura about it. Email them back to let them know it was received, and we'll get back to them once we review the terms."

He hangs up and slides the phone into his pocket.

"Well?" I ask, only making him laugh harder at my impatience.

"Well, Blackwell sent us settlement terms for the case between your brother and Rennensberg High School, and they want to settle for just under six million."

My entire body turns to ice. "Come again? I don't think I heard you correctly."

He just laughs harder. "What's more, is that, since they have no way to reach out to you directly, my receptionist has been fielding requests all morning to have you travel to other states and appear on talk shows, news interviews, and the works."

*This is all so much, so fast.* "Vassago, I don't–"

He puts his palms up. "You don't need to decide right now, but safe to say we need to get you some personnel to help manage this."

I just nod. "What are your recommendations?"

There's a moment of silence, and he tilts his head thoughtfully. "Why don't you tell me what you want to do, and I'll tell you if it matches my recommendations."

If I don't settle with Blackwell, it'll be a long trial, and Cole could be targeted while we try to get justice. If I do settle with Blackwell, it could free up some of that time, give us passive income, and we could travel like I'd hoped to while doing these interviews, although the terms might dictate what I can't say about Cole's case. That could either help or hinder us...

"Depends on the terms... but as long as they don't cause issues for the interviews, I'd say settlement and the works."

Vassago just grins. "I'd say that's a wonderful idea."

# Chapter 42

*Eight Months Later*

"Please remember to behave." I whisper to Cole, and he just rolls his eyes.

"I'm fifteen now, you know. You don't need to coddle me."

I just grin and ruffle his styled hair as he groans loudly. "Whatever you say, kiddo."

Cole swats me away, and I just laugh as Seir and Vassago walk into the room with Vincent in tow. The two murmur to one another with a grin before Vassago's eyes land on me, and heat flashes across his face.

In the end, we didn't settle the lawsuit, and Blackwell lost when the waiver Cole signed was presented. Guess that's what happens when you have a minor sign a legal document. Among all the other things Vassago picked apart in court, that was the nail in the coffin to prove our case, and because Vassago tied it all into what we went through at Father Arrenault's estate, we were awarded a whopping nine million in damages.

Ever since, we've been travelling across state lines for interviews and talk shows, bringing awareness to how Blackwell monopolized the city. Last night I'd gone shopping for new clothes knowing we were flying, and when I saw this little sun dress, I knew Vassago would like it.

Although, with the look he's giving me now, he might just like it too much.

He steps in close, and crowds my space as he walks me backward, around the corner and down the hall, before backing us into a room. He shuts the door with his foot as I faintly hear Vince talking to Cole, and Vassago tilts my chin up, pressing his lips to mine.

My arms snake around his neck as he melds the length of his body to mine, forcing me against the wall as he nips at my lower lip. Murmuring in the kitchen continues, and desire swirls in my core as he reaches down to lift my thigh. Hooking my leg around his waist before pinning his hips to mine, he grinds the length of himself against my clit, and swallows my moans.

He repeats the action until I'm soaked, and panting, grinding my hips to his in a desperate attempt to chase my cresting orgasm. Vassago must know how close I am as he reaches down to lift my other thigh, and suspends me in the air as he supports my ass with his palms.

He's so hard that he's burst through the zipper on his pants, and forced the tip of his dick, his boxers and my underwear as deep as possible. The pressure squeezes my clit even more, and when I moan into his mouth, he thrusts hard. A tearing sound fills the air and with the resistance gone, he hungrily slams into me.

My back bites into the wall as he teases my nipple through my dress. My orgasm comes to a head, and as my body clamps down on him, he shudders, squeezing me further onto his dick as he comes.

We're panting, breathing each other's air, and I'm nearly certain he's covered in come, but that doesn't seem to bother him as he eases me back down, pressing tender kisses along my neck to my lips.

"Seir is going to murder me if we aren't ready to go soon." He presses another kiss to my lips and I nod. "But I think it's a good trade for me to stay here."

I laugh and shove him back an inch before glancing down at the tear in his boxers and the glistening spot on his pants as he tucks himself back in and shrugs. "It could be a souvenir for the day?"

Shaking my head, I point toward our bedroom. "Change."

He places his palm between us. "Fine. Underwear."

Shimmying the torn material down my legs and placing it in his hand, he groans. "Okay, **this** is the souvenir to get me through the day."

I laugh, feeling like come is about to drip down my legs any second. "Okay, go, before Seir gets stabby."

He grins and whirls away toward the room as I slip into the bathroom to clean up. By the time I'm done and in the kitchen, Cole rolls his eyes sarcastically and Vince moves to the door.

Seir glances between us with a knowing look in his eye before ushering everyone outside, and we climb into the vehicle. As we pull away from the house, I can't help but feel like my heart is more full than it's ever been before.

And it's all because of a certain prince of hell.

# Acknowledgements

I have to first, again, say a huge thank you to Amanda Dumky for the insanely gorgeous cover. I will forever appreciate your immense talent more than you will ever possibly know.

A huge thank you to my husband, who supports all my chaotic hobbies, endeavors and passions without a second thought. I love you to the moon and back. In all the romances I write, there's always so many layers of the devotion and undying love that you surround me with that inspires these connections, and I will never take that for granted.

Thank you to my street team for being so supportive, hyping me up even when I was lost in the sauce, and always bringing excitement to my life. You are all beautiful humans and I cannot tell you how thankful I am to have you all in my life.

Lastly, much like with my Unbroken series, thank you to all the readers who decided to give this new series a chance. I can't promise it's the most well written, or well written at all... but I, as with many authors, put a piece of myself into my work, and taking the time to read it... well that may be the best gift of all.

It's just my hope that you enjoyed it, even if only for a moment before you move on to your next adventure.

# Other Works by Aella C Grey

**The Unbroken Series**
>Shadows of Dusk (Unbroken Book 1)
>Light of Dawn (Unbroken Book 2)

**Prince of Hell Series**
>Summoned (Prince of Hell Book 1)
>Barred (Prince of Hell Book 2)
>Convalesced (Prince of Hell Book 3)
>Syndicated (Prince of Hell Book 4)
>Classified (Prince of Hell Book 5)

**Eclipsed Souls Series**
>Wings of Doubt (Eclipsed Souls Book 1)
>Obsidian Flames (Eclipsed Souls Book 2)
>Ascent of the Fallen (Eclipsed Souls Book 3)